2/4

PREGNANT
AT ACOSTA'S
DEMAND

PREGNANT AT ACOSTA'S DEMAND

BY

MAYA BLAKE

HarperCollins
PUBLISHERS
Since 1817

First published in Great Britain 2017
By Mills & Boon, an imprint of HarperCollins*Publishers*
1 London Bridge Street, London, SE1 9GF

Large Print edition 2017

© 2017 Maya Blake

ISBN: 978-0-263-07167-2

MIX
Paper from
responsible sources
FSC
www.fsc.org   FSC° C007454

This book is produced from independently certified FSC paper to ensure responsible forest management. For more information visit www.harpercollins.co.uk/green.

Printed and bound in Great Britain
by CPI Group (UK) Ltd, Croydon, CR0 4YY

To Sandy Baron,
the perfect next-door neighbour.
Thank you for your invaluable support
over the years.

CHAPTER ONE

'DON'T LOOK NOW, but the stuff of your torrid dreams—and my nightmares—just walked in.'

Predictably, at the droll words of caution, Suki Langston's head swivelled towards the entrance of the Ravenswood Arms pub. From their corner booth, she watched the newcomer's incisive gaze sweep the room until it narrowed on reaching them.

Just as predictably, she went from hot to cold. Then blistering hot again as her senses went completely haywire at the sight of Ramon Acosta.

'*Dios mio*, I don't know why I bother.'

She turned back to Luis Acosta, her best friend and the man she held directly responsible for her current state of breathlessness. 'Yes, why do you? You didn't have to tell me he was here!'

He caught her hands in his and gripped them tight, his hazel eyes mercilessly teasing. 'I was trying to spare myself the woeful spectacle of watching you jump and twitch like a cornered mouse when he came up behind you. The last time you two met, I thought you were going to swallow your tongue and spit out your spleen at the same time.'

Heat punched up her face. 'Why do I tolerate you? You're a horrible, horrible human being.'

He laughed and held on tighter when she tried to pull away.

'You tolerate me because by some cosmic stroke of genius we were born on the same day and even though you face-planted in my lap the first time we met at uni, I'm also the best thing that's happened to you since… I don't know…for ever?' Luis replied, his tone extra dry as he waggled his eyebrows at her.

'Are you going to ever let me forget that? Or the fact that you saved me from Professor Winton's roasting the first day of Business Studies because I hadn't drawn up my pre-class plan yet?'

'Let's not forget the numerous times I've saved that pretty behind since then. Which is why I still think you should thank me by coming to work for my family firm.'

'And have you in my ear all day? No, thanks. I enjoy working for Chapman Interiors because I like designing the interior of *homes*, not five-star hotels.'

He threw out a careless shrug. 'Six-star, but who's counting? Whatever, you'll come round one day.'

'Your crystal ball telling you tales again?'

'I don't need one. Just like I don't need a magic ball to tell me you would get on so much better with Ramon if you dealt head-on with that crush that's flattening you—'

'I don't have a crush on him, Luis!' she hissed, darting a frantic look over her shoulder.

Luis sighed dramatically. 'Sure you don't. I think I'm going to change your nickname from mouse to ostrich.'

'Do that and I'll change yours from friend to ass.'

He shrugged. 'I've been called worse.'

Suki watched his gaze move over her shoulder, then return to hers, a resolute look that always made her hackles rise entering his eyes. 'Whatever crazy ideas you're thinking of, burn them now,' she muttered urgently.

He stared at her, a slow smile spreading on his face as his fingers curled tighter around hers. 'Don't worry, little mouse, Luis knows best.'

Suki tried to think of some smart comeback, some wicked put-down that would for once put her overconfident friend in his place. But she knew she was fighting a losing battle. Apart from the useless talent of coming up with the perfect retort hours or even days after she needed it, she was also cursed with a shyness gene that chose moments like these to bloom into life and tie her up in knots.

The other reason she couldn't quite think straight was the man who'd entered the pub two minutes ago.

She could feel him approaching, cutting through the thick Friday night crowd with minimum exertion. She didn't need to look to know that people would be moving out of his way, creating whatever path he wished with a simple commanding look from brooding sea-green eyes. She could already smell that incredible mix of dark earthy spice and alpha male that exuded from him. In the past she'd only needed a quick inhalation for it to fill her nostrils, her senses, turn her into a mumbling wreck around him.

She was twenty-five years old today, for goodness' sake, long past the wide-eyed-teenager stage. She needed to act accordingly...emulate a little bit of the sophistication Luis oozed and Ramon commanded from his very fingertips with such effortless ease.

She needed to raise her head. Yes, that was right. Take in the six-foot-four tower of masculine sleekness and suppressed power who'd arrived at their booth. Stop herself from ogling the square, rugged jaw, the sculpted perfection of his face. Meet his gaze—

'Felíz cumpleaños, mi hermano.'

Dear God, he was too much.

A weird sizzle racing down her back, she lowered her head again, swallowing at the sound of that dark, smoky voice caressing the Cuban Spanish words.

'Gracias, although I was beginning to think I'd only get belated birthday congrats from you, seeing as the day is almost over,' Luis replied, a trace of tension twining his sardonic tone.

Ramon's strong, capable hands slid into his pockets. 'It's barely eleven o'clock and I made it, as I said I would,' he said, an even deeper throb of tension in his voice.

Suki's gaze darted up in time to catch his narrow-eyed gaze on their joint hands before it shifted to his brother. After a second, Luis gave a slight grimace and released her before he shrugged.

'In that case, take a seat. I'll go and fetch the champagne I had the bartender put on ice.'

He slid out of his seat, but despite the slight strain between them, the brothers hugged briefly, Ramon murmuring something to his brother Suki didn't quite catch. Luis nodded, his features relaxing as he murmured back.

Face-to-face, their striking resemblance was unmistakable, the only differences being their eyes, Luis's inch shorter height and hair that was a dark chocolate to his brother's jet black. But where Luis's face and stature evoked keenly interested second glances, Ramon's completely captivated, hypnotising every human being who made the mistake of glancing his way.

It was why, several seconds after Luis had left the booth, and despite urging herself otherwise, Suki couldn't look up. She tightened her hold on the glass holding her wine spritzer, willing her fingers not to shake. But reassuring herself that he was mere flesh and blood seemed utterly useless.

Her breath emerged hard and choppy, when, contrary to her thinking he'd take Luis's seat, he slid into the booth next to her.

Another minute crawled excruciatingly by. A minute when the power of his fixed gaze burned her averted face, when every nerve screamed at being the object of his scrutiny.

'*Felíz cumpleaños*, Suki.'

Unlike the birthday wish he'd delivered to his brother, this one held a little extra…something. Hot and mysterious. Dark and dangerous. Or was it just her stupid, fevered imagination? A shiver went through her. She managed to free one hand from around her glass, long enough to tuck her hair behind her ear before it returned to its death grip around her drink. 'Thank you,' she murmured.

'It's the done thing to look a person in the eyes, at least once, when they're talking to you, is it not?' he drawled. 'Or is your drink infinitely more interesting than I am?'

'It is… I mean…it's the done thing, yes, not my drink—'

'Suki.' Her name was a rigid demand.

One she couldn't have denied even if she'd wanted to. And absurdly, now she was commanded, she didn't have any qualms about turning her head, meeting the gleaming, intense green eyes that focused on her.

She'd met Ramon Acosta a handful of times over the last three years. From the first time when Luis had introduced them at their university graduation ceremony and every occasion since, she'd been struck progressively speechless. Because almost impossibly, her best friend's older brother grew more captivating, the force of his raw magnetism intensifying every time she saw him. Far from Luis's tireless mocking acting as the impetus she needed to kill her senseless crush, her traitorous emotions heightened and sparked even more explosively with each meeting, the stern talking-to she gave herself before each meeting a useless exercise once in Ramon's presence.

It was becoming a problem. But not one she wanted to deal with right now. It was her birthday, after all.

Besides, even if Ramon Acosta were anywhere in her league, he would still be out of bounds on account of his very public, very serious engagement to Svetlana Roskova, the drop-dead gorgeous Russian model.

But, having met his gaze, she couldn't look away. Couldn't think beyond the affirmation of how completely irresistible he was. From the olive-toned vibrancy of his skin to the strong column of the throat exposed by the top two buttons left undone in his dark navy shirt, to the slim fingers resting dangerously close to hers, she was absorbed by him.

'There you are,' he murmured, a trace of dark satisfaction in his voice that triggered alarm within her. 'I'm infinitely pleased that I don't have to spend the rest of the night addressing your profile.'

'You are?' she blurted, then cringed.

Seriously, get a hold of yourself!

One side of his full mouth tilted upward, although Suki didn't spot a single scrap of mirth on his face. 'Contrary to what is widely believed, it turns out that looking into the whites of someone's eyes doesn't guarantee insight into their true nature, but I still prefer that mode of communication.'

This time she caught a definite thread of bitterness, wrapped in thinly veiled fury. 'Is...is something wrong?' she ventured. 'You seem agitated.'

The mocking laugh was unexpected. 'Do I?' he enquired lazily.

His tone grated, morphing, perhaps fortunately, her bemusement to irritation. 'You find my concern amusing?'

Dark green eyes tracked her face, lingered on her mouth. 'Is that what this thing is I'm sensing from you, little mouse? *Concern?*'

'What else could it be? And I wish you two wouldn't call me that,' she replied sharply. 'I'm not a mouse.'

His eyes narrowed again, the trace of distemper thickening. 'Far be it from me to be as predictable as my brother. Rest assured, I will fashion a suitable moniker for you.'

'Or you can use my given name, like everyone else, and just call me Suki?'

For some reason, the request made him tenser. He stilled, his eyes growing even more intense, scrutinising her from forehead to jaw to throat. '*Sí.* I guess I could, Suki,' he rasped.

Her name rolled like an unexploded sensual grenade off his lips, tumbling to a charged stop between them. She stared at him, fighting to breathe, watched his gaze drop and linger for long, unnerving seconds on her mouth. Time ticked away. It might have been a minute. It might have been five. The noise of the pub receded but she could hear his steady breathing, feel the condensation from the glass coating her fingers, the cold a deep contrast to the fire burning inside her.

'Are you and my brother involved?' The question was grim and rapier-sharp.

'Involved?' she parroted, still caught in the grip of the electrical storm brewing between them. 'I don't know what—'

'You wish me to be explicit? Are you screwing my brother?' he demanded.

She exhaled in a horrified little rush. 'Excuse me?'

'Pretended outrage at my language isn't necessary. A simple *yes* or *no* will suffice.'

Another healthy bout of irritation flared, saving her jumbled senses. 'I'm not sure what's up with you, but you obviously woke up on the wrong side of the bed today, so—'

The low curse was uttered in Spanish, but she knew it was potent nevertheless. 'Indulge me and let's refrain from the mention of beds and who woke up where for the moment, *cara*.'

She frowned. 'Well, you're sort of proving my point with that statement. Which begs the question why did you come here to celebrate your brother's birthday if you're in such a terrible mood?'

The skin bracketing his mouth pinched white as his nostrils flared. Suki watched, her spine stiffening with dread as his fist balled on the table. 'Because I'm *loyal*. Because when I give my word I keep it. Because Luis trusts me to be there for him and it's my duty to honour that trust.'

The icy fury with which he delivered the words robbed her of breath, but only for a moment. 'I wasn't questioning your loyalty or—'

'You still haven't answered my question.'

She shook her head, struggling to follow the mercurial swing of the conversation. 'Probably because it's none of your business.'

His fist tightened further. 'You think it's none of my business? When he treats you like you belong to him but you look at me with those gorgeous, *greedy* blue eyes?'

She gasped, her insides clenching tight with mortification. 'I don't!'

His laughter was mocking and cruel. 'You pretended you needed the encouragement to acknowledge me, but your eyes haven't stopped devouring me since I sat down. Fair warning though, even as much as Luis means to me, I don't share my women. *Ever.* So a *ménage à trois* will be out of the question.'

'I... God, you're despicable,' she replied, horror dredging through her, because he'd not only so easily witnessed the stupid feelings she'd been desperate to hide, but had also felt no qualms about calling her out on them.

'Am I? Or are you just disappointed because whatever hot little scenario you concocted in your head has been rumbled?'

'Believe me, I have no earthly idea what you're talking about. And I'm sorry if someone misplaced a few of your billions or kicked your puppy because clearly something's happened today to put you in this filthy mood. But, regardless of that, *I* should warn *you* that I'm two seconds from throwing my drink in your face. So unless you want a cold drenched body to go with that deplorable attitude, I suggest you shut up right now! And also, how dare you speak to me of sharing and...and *ménages*? Aren't you *engaged* to—?'

'*Madre de Dios*, how long was I away for?' Luis slid into the seat and nodded thanks to the waitress who set the ice bucket and champagne flutes down. 'Because I could've sworn it was only five minutes. And yet you two look like you're about to come to blows? I'm surprised at you, little mouse.' Although his tone was jovial, his eyes were shrewd as they slid from her to his brother.

Suki shook her head, unable to believe what was happening. 'Trust me, I'm not—'

'I was setting your girlfriend straight on a few things,' Ramon interjected.

Luis's eyebrows shot up, then he laughed. 'My *girlfriend*? Where did you get that idea?'

Silence reigned at the table. Suki glared at her supposed best friend.

Ramon's tight jaw eased a fraction before he shrugged. 'Are you saying she doesn't belong to you?'

Suki's teeth clenched. *'Excuse—?'*

'Sí, she belongs to me—'

'Can you please stop talking about me as if I'm some ornament?' she interrupted.

Ramon ignored her, his keen gaze fixed on his brother.

Luis's lighter eyes narrowed. 'Like a sister belongs to a brother who cares for her. Like a friend owns the entitlement of kicking *someone's* ass if they so much as whisper a threat of harm her way. Like—'

'Understood,' Ramon said, his voice firm and grave.

'Good, I'm glad that's settled,' Luis replied, then reached for the champagne.

Suki turned her head, met the newly gleaming gaze Ramon turned on her. 'Is it? Is it *settled*?' she hissed.

One corner of his mouth quirked, as if now his brother had explained he found the whole subject amusing. 'I got the wrong end of the stick, it seems, *gatito*.'

'Is that supposed to be an apology?' she snapped.

A fleeting expression darkened his eyes. 'Permit me some time to find the right words.'

Considering Ramon Acosta was lauded worldwide as possessing the Midas touch with every venture he turned his hand to, she found it impossible to believe he was lost for anything.

He'd single-handedly turned his parents' half a dozen Cuban-based hotels into the world-renowned Acosta International Hotels chain while pursuing a private but deeply passionate artistic talent. When Svetlana Roskova had accidentally on purpose let slip during an interview that she was a muse for, and involved with, an artist, the media had clamoured to know who had won the heart of the Russian beauty.

After several sources had speculated that it was indeed Ramon, he'd given a single exclusive interview confirming himself as her lover and the man behind the wildly successful Piedra Galleries. Overnight, his already highly sought after paintings and sculptures had become priceless collectors' items, with commissions from monarchs and world leaders placed on a waiting list that stretched into years, according to Luis.

But the man Suki had placed on a lofty pedestal was far removed from the one now watching her with wild, unsettling eyes. A fact his own brother noted as he peeled the foil off the champagne cork.

'You seem wound up tighter than normal, Ramon. I can virtually see the smoke curling from your ears. It's quite a sight to behold,' Luis observed dryly.

Ramon's mouth tightened. 'Is this how you wish to spend the rest of your birthday, lobbing jokes at me?' he asked without taking his eyes off Suki.

She suppressed a shiver, wondering what was going on behind the hooded green eyes.

'I was just trying to lighten this heavier than normal mood, seeing as it's *my* birthday and I can do what I want, but if you're not going to explain yourself, at least answer that damn phone that's been buzzing in your pocket for the last five minutes?'

Ramon shifted his gaze from her long enough to flick his brother an impatient look before reaching into his jacket. Extracting the sleek phone from his pocket, he barely glanced at it before powering it off.

Luis's jaw dropped. 'You're *actually* turning off the power source to the empire? Are you unwell? Or are you ignoring someone specific?'

'Luis…' His voice held patent warning. One his younger brother didn't heed.

'*Dios*, is there trouble in paradise? Has the great Svetlana tripped over her stilettos and fallen from grace?'

Ramon Acosta's face iced up, his eyes turning a shade of turbulent green. 'I was waiting until later to share the news, but if you must know, as of this morning, I'm no longer engaged.'

He was no longer engaged.

As if his words had caused the planet to stop turning, silence descended on the booth. The three of them remained frozen in place, even as the words ricocheted through her brain.

He was no longer engaged.

Suki jumped at the sound of the cork forcefully ejecting from the bottle. Frothy, expensive liquid spilled. The sounds and smell of the pub roared back into her consciousness. But still the words pounded through her head.

Ramon was no longer committed to another woman.

She frowned at the giddy relief swirling through her, then started as a flute of champagne was thrust into her hands.

'Drink up, little mouse. Now we have two…no, *three* reasons to celebrate,' Luis said, eyeing her with even deeper resolution.

'I'm glad my broken engagement brings you such sublime joy, *hermano*,' Ramon replied, his voice arctic cold.

Luis sobered. 'I chose to respect your relationship, but my views on your engagement never changed. She was the wrong woman for you. Whether the move to end it was hers or yours—'

'It was mine.'

Luis's smile returned. 'Then either celebrate with me or drown your sorrows. Either way, we're finishing this champagne.' He poured two more glasses.

Ramon waited a beat, then raised his glass and recited another clipped birthday toast before tossing back the drink. Luis, his point made, proceeded to drink most of the bottle, while Suki sipped hers.

All the while tension reigned, heightened even further by the looks Ramon kept casting her way.

She breathed a sigh of relief when Luis rose just after midnight, his predatory gaze on a stunning redhead smiling at him from two seats away.

'Time to make a significant start on my second quarter-century.'

Suki pushed away her half-finished glass. 'I think I'll head home—'

'Stay,' Ramon said. Before she could reply, he turned to his brother. 'My limo is outside. Have the driver deliver you wherever you want to go.'

Luis clapped his hand on his brother's shoulder. 'I appreciate the offer but I'm going to tread delicately with this flower. We don't want her overwhelmed and bolting at the sight of all those Acosta billions before I get the chance to close the deal, now, do we?'

Ramon's jaw tightened before he shrugged. 'Very well. I'll leave you to serenade your paramour on the night bus.'

'*Dios*, everything is such an extreme with you, isn't it? There's such a thing as a black cab, you know? And even with the lowly salary you pay me as junior marketing executive, I can still afford one.'

'If you say so. Either way, I expect you to report to the office sober and whole on Monday morning.'

'As long as *you* promise to deliver Suki home, safe and sound.'

She shook her head, grabbing her handbag as she rose. 'There's no need. I'll be fine getting home by myself.' Although she *would* be relying on the maligned public transport, the reason to keep a close eye on her spending casting a sudden grey shadow on her birthday. Her phone hadn't rung in the four hours since she'd called the hospital to check on her mother so she must be having a relatively restful night. At least she hoped so.

'Sit down, Suki,' Ramon drawled, his tone throbbing with implacable power. 'You and I aren't finished.'

She ignored him. Or at least she tried. She cast a desperate look towards Luis, but her friend merely reached across the table and hugged her close, murmuring in her ear, 'It's your birthday, Suki. Life's too short. Give yourself a break and live a little. It'll make you happy, and it'll make me infinitely ecstatic!'

Before she could respond, he was headed for the redhead's table, smiling that smile that made women trip over themselves.

'I said, sit down,' Ramon pressed.

There was no way to leave the booth while he blocked her exit. With Luis's words ringing in her ears, she slowly sank back into her seat. 'I can't imagine why you'd want me to. I have nothing more to say to you.'

His gaze gradually defrosted from arctic cold to heated green as he scrutinised her face with that unnerving intensity. 'I think we established that I owe you...something.'

'An *apology*. Is that a difficult word for you to say?'

He shrugged and opened his mouth, just as raucous laughter fuelled by hours' long hard drinking erupted from a group nearby.

Distaste crossing his face, he rose and stationed himself at the mouth of the booth. 'Come, we'll continue this conversation elsewhere.'

Despite his imperious tone, Suki stood, telling herself she was obeying just so she could make a quick getaway once they were outside. Ramon Acosta had revealed a part of himself tonight that scraped her giddy dreams raw. She'd seen the ruthless man the financial papers wrote about, the insufferable deity-like brother Luis complained about. She'd also seen a bitter man turned lethally furious by his broken engagement.

Whatever had happened between Ramon and

Svetlana still pulsed ill-feeling through his veins. Even now, she felt him loom like a dark lord behind her, quiet fury pouring off him.

The glimpse into his character was a timely reminder that Suki grabbed and held close. Her experiences of men, including her own father, had left her with a deeply ingrained distrust that, unfortunately, received further validation with each interaction with the opposite sex.

Thus far, Luis was the only one who'd breached that distrust. He was the reason why, believing there were other exceptions like him, she'd attempted, despite her mother's bitter warnings about men, to date six months ago.

Stephen turning out to be a two-timing louse had left her hurt, but not surprised. The part of her that still stung now warned her that whatever was going on with Ramon, she wanted no part of it.

Exiting the pub into brisk October air, she breathed in deep. And started to walk away.

A firm hand caught her elbow before she'd taken three steps, dragging her to a halt. 'Where do you think you're going?' Ramon breathed.

With the sounds of the pub now in the background, her every sense was filled with him. She took a step back, fighting the insane sensations that warred inside her. He tracked her move, crowding her with his smell, his overwhelming body, that ferocious look in his eyes.

Much too much. Despite the pathetic weakening in her limbs, she met his gaze. 'It's late.'

'I'm aware of the time of night,' he murmured, moving closer, brushing her legs with his.

The weakness intensified. 'I need to… I should go.'

He took another step forward, bracing both hands either side of her head and trapping her against the pub wall. '*Sí*, perhaps you *should*. But you don't want to.'

She shook her head, frantically calling on her common sense. 'Yes, I do.'

He leaned closer, until she could see the tiny gold flecks in his eyes, feel the warm, faintly champagne-tinged breath on her face. 'You can't. I've yet to give you my apology.'

'So you admit to owing me one?'

His gaze dropped to her mouth, spiky hunger that fused with hers flaring in his eyes. 'Yes, but I'm not giving it to you here.'

She managed the almost impossible feat of laughing. 'You know what birthday I'm celebrating so you *know* I wasn't born yesterday.'

One hand left the wall, his fingers drifting down her cheek. 'I can tell you what you want to hear right here and you can walk away. Or you can let me take you home as I promised Luis I would while giving you that apology. Surely you want to give your friend that peace of mind?'

She shook her head against the magic he was weaving with his low, husky voice and sizzling touch. 'I'm a big girl. Luis will understand. All I want is that apology,' she insisted.

'You want more than that. You want to give in, reach out and take that forbidden thing you've been craving for a while now. Don't you, Suki?'

No.

She opened her mouth, but the word stalled in her throat.

Ramon pushed away from the wall, took a bold step back, then another, robbing her of his closeness, dangling the possibility of loss in her face.

No.

This time the word was in objection of the temptation she knew she shouldn't surrender to. Suki wasn't aware she'd followed him to the edge of the kerb until a sleek black limo rolled to a stop behind him. Reaching for the handle, he pulled the door open, his eyes not leaving her face. 'You will get in the car and I'll take you home, Suki. What happens beyond that will be up to you. Only you.'

CHAPTER TWO

INSTINCTIVELY SHE KNEW her path was set the moment she murmured, 'Okay.'

Life's too short. Give yourself a break and live a little.

Suki knew that there would be no turning back the second she let Ramon help her into the car and he slid along the soft leather bench seat after her. The door slammed behind them, cocooning them in silence and edgy lust.

'Your address?' he rasped.

'167 Winston Street, Vauxhall.'

He relayed the information to the driver, then his mouth firmed. 'There are two dozen pubs between where you live and Luis's residence in Mayfair. Why do you choose one so far outside of the city?' he asked, casting an irritated glance at the establishment that stood on a quiet street in the middle of Watford.

'A uni friend of ours just inherited it from his parents. Luis promised we'd stop by for birthday drinks,' she said, a little relieved at the harmless tone of the conversation.

He'd activated the privacy partition and tinted the back windows, and now, trapped in the dark expanse of the luxurious car, his scent once again sliding intimately over her senses, she needed something to alleviate it.

Unfortunately, the reprieve didn't last long. 'And do you always do what my brother says?' he asked, a different type of edge lining his voice.

Her fingers tightened around the strap of her handbag. 'Are you about to pick another fight with me? Because if I recall, we haven't resolved the last one to my satisfaction yet.'

In the space of one breath and the next, he closed the gap between them. Her bag was plucked from her fingers and tossed onto the adjacent seat. Firm fingers speared into her hair, the grip firm enough to direct her gaze up to his.

Electricity vibrated from his body, the dark, purposeful gleam in his eyes rendering her mouth dry. He stared down at her for an age, their breaths mingling.

'*Lo siento.* I'm sorry for my less than admirable assumptions. I am not in the best mood tonight, but that was no excuse, so accept my apologies.'

The words were deep and genuine, momentarily

silencing the voice screaming a warning at her. 'I… Okay,' she mumbled.

His fingers moved, slowly massaging her scalp in lazy, masterful rotations, triggering a low heat in her belly. 'Are you satisfied?' he asked.

'That…that depends.'

One eyebrow rose but the rest of his face tautened with expectation. 'On what?'

'On whether or not you're about to start another fight with me.'

'No, *querida*,' he breathed. 'I'm about to start something else entirely. And you know it.'

'I don't…'

'Enough, Suki. I told you what happens next is up to you. But I get the feeling I need to move things along before one of us expires from impatience. So the only word I want out of that delectable mouth right now is *yes* or *no*. I want you, *gatito*. Do you want me? Regardless of my sub-exemplary behaviour tonight. Yes or no?'

Her heart leapt into her throat. For three long years she'd harboured a growing crush on this man. But nowhere in that secret longing had there been a possibility that he would be here, in front of her, saying these words to her. She'd always believed she would wake up one day to find herself cured. She'd dated a handful of men like Stephen who, even before they'd proved themselves faithless, had fallen victim to not being *dynamic* enough, *confident* enough, tall enough or dark enough—hell, even *Spanish* enough.

Stephen's betrayal had triggered a numbness of her emotions, had finally pressed home every warning her mother had relayed since she turned sixteen. A desperate part of her wished for that numbness now, yearned for a clap of thunder to deliver her from the ferocious lust threatening to swallow her whole.

Because, staring into Ramon Acosta's eyes, she didn't think she was anywhere near numb. Anywhere near cured of her foolish crush.

And now that he was free...

Oh, God.

She shook her head; the voice whispering that this was the worst idea she'd ever had grew into a scream. Swallowing, she slicked her tongue over her lower lip.

His fingers convulsed in her hair and a strangled sound escaped his throat. About to utter the word that would free her from this madness, she dropped her gaze. His velvet-smooth lips were so close. And good heavens, she was so hungry for a taste.

One. Just one.

Then she would satisfy herself that he was no god, that the lofty status she'd afforded him in her mind was nothing more than dreams spun from loneliness and long-forgotten fairy tales.

'Suki.' Her name was a fierce, demanding whisper. A silken, alluring chain winding her closer.

Her breasts grew heavy, the slick, damp place between her thighs clenching with a manic need she'd never experienced before.

'Yes.' The word poured from her in a swell of surrender.

Ramon didn't need further encouragement. With a rough exhalation, he tugged her closer to meet his descending mouth. A hot, demanding mouth that slanted over hers, fusing power and pleasure into her fired-up senses.

His tongue stroked against her lips, tasting boldly, over and over before he demanded entrance. Entrance she gave with a shaky wonder at the thought that she was kissing Ramon Acosta. That wonder melted away in the next instance when he licked his way into her mouth.

Sensation lashed her from head to toe, the onslaught eliciting helpless whimpers that started from deep within and were crushed between their melded lips. The knowledge that she was whimpering sent another bolt of shock through her. She'd been kissed before. Enough times to know that no one kiss was the same, that some were better than others.

But *nothing* compared to the kiss Ramon was delivering now. Each slide of his tongue against hers, each bold nip of her swelling flesh rained sizzling delight on her, making her strain closer, silently pleading for more.

When the need to breathe forced them apart, he only permitted a second, smoothing his thumb across her lips in a hungry caress. '*Dios mio*, you taste incredible,' he growled before he took her mouth again, unbelievably deepening the kiss.

The words freed her from a hold she wasn't even aware of, the guttural utterance lending her enough feminine confidence to unfold her hands from the death grip on the seat. To raise one hand and settle it on his thigh.

He tensed, hard muscles bunching beneath her hand. He tore his mouth from hers to spear her with a rabid look, the light in his eyes sending a thread of apprehension down her spine. Not the kind that made her fear for her safety. The kind that informed her he was stroking the edge of his sensual limits and was determined to take her down with him.

She started to move her hand. He caught and

trapped it against his heated flesh, his eyes flashing as he stared down at her. 'You want to touch me, then touch me.'

'Ramon...'

He inhaled sharply. 'I think this is the first time I've heard you say my name.'

'I...what?' It couldn't be. She'd said it so many times...*in her fantasies.*

The hold in her hair propelled her closer. 'Say it again,' he breathed against her lips.

'Ramon,' she whispered feverishly.

A light tremble vibrated through him. Diving back down, he sealed his mouth to hers. The hand covering hers released her to slide up her arm, stopping every few inches to explore her bare skin. Halfway up, he changed course, his caress gliding over her hip to her waist to the underside of her breast. It stayed here, tantalisingly close to the needy weight that yearned to be touched, the nipples that screamed for attention.

Her breath hitched as hunger ploughed through her. Beneath her hand, his thigh shifted, demanding her attention. She caressed him through the material of his expensive tailored trousers. Higher. To the enormous bulge behind his zipper. And froze at his tight, tormented groan.

'No. Don't stop, *querida*. Touch me,' he commanded against her mouth.

She smoothed her hand over him, tightened her fist against his virile girth. Thick, inflamed Spanish words spilled from his lips, bruising her mouth with their heat. When one ravenous hand cupped her breast, squeezed and tortured, she returned the words with needful moans. One lane of pleasure rolled into the other, delirium swelling high as he moulded and caressed and kissed.

Suki wasn't sure when he pushed her back against the leather upholstery or when he tugged her hips to the edge of the bench seat. Not sure when the side zip of her black wool dress was lowered or when he pushed up the hem. But at some point between one potent kiss and the next, he was on his knees between her thighs, his hands sliding up her legs, over the silk stockings she'd treated herself to in a mad moment of weakness last weekend. More fevered words spilled when he encountered their lace tops.

His fingers traced over them, then trailed over her bare skin. A shudder raked her from head to toe. With one last forceful kiss, he raised his head.

'I need to see you, Suki,' he rasped, his voice barely recognisable. His hip flexed against her hold, the power of his erection thickening in her hand. 'Touch you as you are touching me.'

At the back of her mind a warning blazed. A kiss. This was supposed to be *just a kiss*.

But already her head was moving in a nod, her blood thrilling to the new, unexpected turn the night had taken. There was no way what was happening between them would be sustainable beyond tonight. For one thing, she was too emotionally bruised, her instinct even now shocked at her behaviour. For another, her mother needed her.

Lastly, Ramon divided his time between the many Acosta hotels and his homeland of Cuba. The likelihood of her seeing him again for a very long time, especially once Luis took over the New York flagship hotel, as he was being groomed for, would be low to nil.

And despite the insanity of the sensations Ramon evoked in her now, she knew the shine would wear off sooner rather than later. So maybe she would allow more than just a kiss. Maybe, she would heed Luis's words, and live a little. Just for tonight—

The fingers tracing the outer edge of her satin and lace panties dragged her back to the exhilarating present. To the looming presence of the powerful man crouched over her.

'I must be losing my touch if your mind chooses

this moment to go for a wander. What were you thinking about?' he demanded, his thumb sliding dangerously close to her sex.

She shivered. 'I…nothing.'

He doubled the caress with a thumb on the other side. 'Don't lie to me, Suki. I've had enough of those in the last twenty-four hours. Were you thinking of another man?' he sliced at her, his nostrils flaring with quiet fury. 'While you lay ready and open for me, were you thinking of someone else? A boyfriend, perhaps?'

Her eyes widened and she tried to scramble away. She didn't succeed because he refused to let her go. 'You think I'd be here, like this with you if I had a boyfriend?'

'Answer the question, Suki,' he challenged, his tone growing even more arctic.

She shook her head. 'No, I don't have a boyfriend. If…you must know I was thinking of you.'

The tension gripping him eased. His eyes gleamed. 'What exactly were you thinking?' he probed as his thumbs slid under the thin barrier and caressed her damp flesh.

A moan ripped free, her shaky exhalation rushing through her lips. 'That I won't see you again after tonight.'

He stilled. His fingers dug into her. Eyes turned

almost black regarded her in abrasive silence. 'And is that what you want? For us to use each other for one single night and forget the other one exists come morning?' There was something darkly condemning in his voice, but also enough sexual anticipation that said he wasn't completely averse to that scenario. The opposing forces of that view left her speechless, unable to decide which one would most please him.

He leaned in closer, bringing his power and might to bear on her. 'Answer me, Suki. Is that what you want?' Blade-sharp eyes searched hers.

'Isn't it what you want too?' She forced a laugh. 'Please don't tell me you see anything more beyond...whatever this is happening tonight?'

He was silent for an interminable age. Then his gaze dropped to her shoulders and upper breasts exposed by the gaping dress. Lower to the rapid rise and fall of her torso. To the restless hands on the seat beside her hips, twitching with the need to touch him. Finally to her splayed legs and the black panties whose thin, insubstantial material framed her core. His thumbs caressed again, drawing another shameless shudder from her.

'*Sí*, you're right. Nothing more can come out of this. Nothing *will*.'

The sharp dart of hurt somewhere deep beneath

her breastbone disappeared at the pleasure pain of her panties cutting into her flesh one moment, then ripping free of her body the next.

Suki gasped, the move so audaciously erotic, she felt her folds dampen further.

Ramon's eyes remained on her for a further intense second. Then they dropped to her core.

Heat scoured his cheekbones, his lips parting as he breathed her in. She wasn't sure whether it was the sight of him on his knees before her or the power of sensations ploughing through her. But the urge to touch him grew too big to contain. She cupped his jaw, slid her hand along over the masculine stubble to his strong throat, then around to his nape. A tight smile whispered over his lips, gone in the next breath.

Then he was lowering his head, his intent very clear. Her grip tightened, pulling him away, her eyes widening at the blatant act he was about to perform.

'Ramon, I don't...' she started. Her train of thought dissolved at the firm kiss he delivered to her core, her fingers convulsing in his hair as pleasure jerked through her. 'Oh!'

Raising his head, he blew gently on her. 'You want me to stop?'

The anxious part of her that had rejected what

he was about to do frantically begged for more. 'No,' she blurted.

At his husky laugh, heat washed up her face.

But laughter and all trace of embarrassment evaporated beneath the deluge of rapture his next kiss brought. He tasted her and pleasured her with bold, possessive strokes, ramping up her pleasure until her eyes rolled in bliss. Until hoarse, alien words fell from her lips and her fingers sank deep into his hair, urging him on, begging for more.

He gave generously, his tongue and lips drawing untold delight from her. When he finally concentrated his attention on her tight, swollen nub, Suki's back arched off the seat, a ragged scream ripping from her throat before her whole body was gripped in wave after wave of ecstasy.

She resurfaced to the scent of sex and leather and the sight of a virile, hungry, half-naked man. He'd disposed of his jacket, his shirt hung half open and his trousers were unzipped. Black luxurious hair looked sexily dishevelled as if someone...*she*... had run her hands through it in mindless caresses.

Her barely decelerated heartbeat kicked up again as she watched him slide on a condom with one hand and roughly push down her dress and free her arms with the other. Next, he unclipped and eased off her bra.

At the sight of her exposed full breasts, he swore low and hard. '*Santa cielo*, you're exquisite.'

As if testing the reality of her skin, he smoothed his hand down from her neck to her stomach, bypassing the needy, screaming peaks of her breasts. On the upward caress, his other hand left his sheathed manhood. Both hands cupped her breasts, his thumbs mercilessly teasing her nipples for a mindless stretch of time before he sucked one into his mouth. Hard on the heels of her expended climax, renewed pleasure surged. High and heady and unthinkably surreal.

Was she really here, about to—?

'*Oh, God,*' she moaned, her mind fracturing as he grazed his teeth over her nipple.

Still torturing her, he wrapped one arm around her waist and dragged her lower until her buttocks hung off the seat. She was a heartbeat from tossing herself over another cliff into another mind-blowing climax when he lifted his head.

Fervid green eyes met and trapped hers as he drew her legs over his shoulders. Then, with a grunt, he gripped her waist and thrust hard and deep inside her.

Her strangled scream was kissed away, urgent hands holding her in place for his second thrust.

'*Dios*...so wet...so tight.' His voice was gravel-rough hoarse, the words barely coherent.

Suki gave up trying to decipher them, her mind fracturing into useless pieces as she was fully submerged in the fiery enchantment of Ramon's possession. He commanded her body like a masterful virtuoso, driving her to the peak and pinning her there, over and over, but not letting her fall.

As the limo ate up the miles they writhed beneath streetlights thrown intermittently into the car.

'Ramon... Ramon...'

She wasn't sure how many times she moaned his name to his thick encouragement. But she was fully astride his kneeling form, their bodies slick with sweat and his implacable arms around her when he raised his head one final time, looked deep into her eyes and instructed, 'Now, Suki.'

Glorious pleasure and pressure burst wide open. She could do nothing but hang on as it sucked her deep into a bottomless vortex.

He caught her earlobe in a sharp bite a second before he was hurled into his own release, muttering hot, torrid words that drew out her own pleasure as he jerked inside her.

They were still breathing hard when the car swayed round a corner and drew to a stop. He caressed her for another minute before he set her back on the seat and zipped up her dress.

Unable to meet his eyes or stop the flames of disquiet eating her up, Suki snatched up her panties and bra and stuffed them inside her handbag.

Beside her, having straightened his own clothes, Ramon lounged back in the seat.

'Um…thanks for the lift,' she said after a full minute when it became clear he didn't intend to speak.

He didn't reply, just stared at her with hooded dark eyes. *Okay…* Clutching her handbag, she edged closer to the door. 'Goodnight, Ramon. Have a safe trip back to…wherever.'

She reached for the handle. He beat her to it, catching her hand and tugging her round to face him.

'No, I'm not about to have a safe trip back to… *wherever*. Because we're not done, *guapa*. Far from it,' he said.

Exiting the car with the grace of a sleek, powerful animal, he held out his hand to her.

She had no choice but to get out. She knew that. But suddenly what awaited her outside was more daunting than the mind-bending sex she'd just enjoyed in this car. For one thing, her heart and mind hadn't stopped racing. And the voice screeching in her head that this was over and she needed to walk away was growing weaker under the one howling harder in greedy, grabby need. The one telling her she wanted more. *Needed* to live a little for longer. Experience more of what had just happened. Of everything.

'Come out, Suki,' he ordered.

She told herself that she complied because she couldn't stay in the limo for ever. Not because the unabated hunger in his eyes called to hers.

The moment she stepped out, he slammed the door shut and tapped twice on the roof. As the limo pulled away he yanked her close, delivered a hard, searing kiss to her mouth. That single spark was enough to ignite the erotic conflagration again. Long moments later, he raised his head, glanced up at the small Victorian terrace house she called home, then back at her. 'Invite me in.'

She invited him in.

But even before he'd stepped over the threshold into her sanctuary, Suki knew that this was nowhere near the forgettable experience she had convinced herself it would be.

CHAPTER THREE

Ten months later

SUKI READ THE email one more time, the shaking in her hands nothing compared to the pain lacerating her heart as she took in the stark words that blended with soul-breaking ones. Halfway through the first paragraph, her vision blurred. She blinked and tears spilled down her cheeks. Swiping them away, she closed her eyes for a moment, vainly wishing the words would be different when she opened them again.

They weren't.

Private memorial for Luis Acosta and his parents, Clarita and Pablo Acosta. A strictly family affair. Unless expressly invited, please do not attend.

Lawyers request your presence for the reading of his last will and testament followed by a private meeting with Ramon Acosta. Attendance strictly necessary.

Her throat clogging with fresh tears just waiting to be shed, she looked away from the words she didn't want to read, never mind accept, and clicked on the attachment. A slight bolt of shock went through her when it sent her to an airline website. Swallowing, she clicked on further links until she arrived at the page holding the first-class return e-ticket to Cuba under her name.

The email and attachment had come from a firm of lawyers in Havana, the ones she'd been desperate to contact ever since she received the horrendous news of Luis's and his parents' deaths.

The same lawyers who'd refused to take her calls or answer her letters for two months, but were now reaching out to her. She knew they wouldn't have contacted her without the express permission of Ramon Acosta, their client.

This email giving consent for her to visit Cuba to pay her respects wouldn't have come from anyone else because Ramon was the only one left of the Acosta family.

Despite the turn of events after their night together, she'd reached out to him after Luis died. At first Suki had respected his deafening silence, knowing that he was grieving the family he'd tragically lost in a car crash. Until she'd learned via social media that several of their university friends had been invited to attend Luis's funeral three weeks after his death. The date had come and gone without any of her frantic calls being returned by Ramon's office or his lawyers, forcing her to grieve her best friend's burial alone in her bedroom. Every single email she'd sent after that had also gone unanswered.

Until today.

She wanted to hate Ramon for denying her something so fundamental as a goodbye to the only true friend she'd known. But her emotions, already scraped raw by everything she'd endured these past ten months, were too shredded to accommodate another detrimental emotion such as hate.

Although she'd already been through a gamut of them. For weeks, she'd cried, begged, then railed against fate. And science. And her own weak body.

When she'd finally reached acceptance, she'd cried for days. Those tears had sapped the last of her will to fight, dropped her to what she'd foolishly thought was rock bottom. Until Luis was also ripped from her. Then she'd known true devastation.

Devastation she'd had to deal with on her own, while grappling with her own loss and remaining strong for her mother. The multiple blows fate had dealt her still possessed the power to disrupt her sleep and trigger bouts of tearful sadness.

Like when she'd dissolved into floods of tears during her meeting with the head of HR at her workplace last week. Even before she'd finished the return-to-work interview, she knew things hadn't gone well.

Her boss had insisted she take the full three months of her sick leave, the need to protect themselves from professional liability overshadowing her protests that, with only one month remaining, she was ready to return to work.

She'd petitioned. With her finances fast dwindling and her mother's medical bills piling up, she'd appealed the decision and been granted the interview. Only for her overwhelmed state to get the better of her.

She hadn't been surprised when her HR manager had sympathetically ended the interview and called a taxi to take Suki home. What she hadn't expected was a letter a few days later stating that her sick leave had been extended by another month with half pay because she wasn't deemed fit to deal with clients in her current state.

Suki had been too drained to fight the assessment. And deep down she knew that, as much as she loved her job as an interior designer for one of the most prestigious firms in London, her passion had been depleted.

She didn't need a psychologist to tell her she needed to find closure before things got better. Or barring that, a different avenue for the cocktail of emotions bubbling beneath the surface of her heart.

Closing her laptop, she rose from her small desk and trudged to the kitchen to dispose of her barely touched cup of tea. Mechanically, she washed the mug and set it on the draining board.

Outside, birds chirped and wasps buzzed as Vauxhall basked in the August bank holiday sunshine.

Suki turned her back on it, her hand sliding as it so often, so painfully did to her stomach, to the child that had never managed to thrive there. The urge to walk upstairs to her bedroom, curl up under her duvet and slide into perpetual oblivion was almost catatonically irresistible.

She fought the temptation, her mind returning to the email and the airline ticket. Although she'd been prepared to dig into her meagre savings to pay her last respects to her best friend two months ago, her resources had dwindled even further owing to her mother being readmitted to hospital. With confirmation of her cancer, Suki had

had to use almost all her remaining funds to keep her and her mother's heads above water.

Travelling to Cuba had fast become a distant dream.

The arrival of the ticket, although it bruised her pride a little, wasn't one she was about to refuse. For a chance to say goodbye to Luis, she would set aside her ego for the moment. Once she was back at work, she would pay Ramon Acosta back every penny she owed him for the ticket.

The decision eroded a little bit of her apathy, made her half turn back towards the window, allow the sunshine to touch her face. Warm her.

She wasn't aware how long she stood there, making careful plans, her soul mourning the vibrant, charismatic man she'd been lucky enough to call her friend.

The soft beeping on her laptop, reminding her of the appointment at the hospital, finally roused her. On automatic, she dressed, left home and made the short drive to the hospital that held far too many harrowing memories.

Fighting the ravaging pain that attacked her, Suki blocked out the smell of disinfectant and death, forced a smile, and entered her mother's ward.

Moira Langston was dozing lightly, her shrunken form lost in stark white sheets. Sensing Suki's presence, she opened her eyes. For a second, they just stared at each other.

Then her mother gave a soft, shuddering exhalation. 'I told you not to visit. I know how hard it is for you to come here.'

Suki laid her hand over her mother's. 'I'm okay, Mum. It's not that bad,' she lied.

Moira's lips pursed. 'Don't lie. You know I can't bear lies.'

Tension rippled in the air, twisting through pain churning inside them both. Broken trust fired by a thousand lies was what had shattered her mother's heart long before Suki was born. It was the reason Moira Langston had never again let another man close enough to hurt her, the reason she'd drummed into Suki the need to protect her own heart at all costs.

It was the reason her mother had been bitterly angry with her when Suki had told her about her pregnancy. Her mother had come round eventually, even put aside her own health issues to support her after she lost the baby, but the look of mournful regret still lingered.

Suki swallowed, and tightened her grip on her mother's hand. 'I can't *not* visit you, Mum.'

Moira sighed, her face softening. 'I know. But I'm feeling better, so I should be home very soon.'

Suki didn't argue, although her mother's notable weight loss told a different story. They chatted about neutral subjects for a while, before her mother's shrewd eyes settled on her one more time. 'Something's bothering you.'

She started to shake her head, but, not wanting to upset her mother, she took a deep breath. 'I heard from Ra...from Luis's brother's lawyers.'

Moira's eyes narrowed. 'And? What did Ramon have to say for himself?' she demanded sharply.

'I...nothing. The lawyers sent me a ticket to Cuba. To attend Luis's memorial.'

'Are you going to accept it?'

Slowly, she nodded. 'I want to say goodbye properly.'

For a long moment, Moira remained silent. 'Luis was a good man. That's the only reason I won't tell you not to go. But, be careful, Suki. Stay away from his brother. He's caused you enough grief as it is.'

Her mother had been quick to lay the blame for everything at Ramon's feet when she found out Suki was pregnant and alone. Ravaging pain and the need to mourn her lost baby in isolation had made her hold her tongue against telling her mother that Ramon had no knowledge that he'd fathered a baby. That was an assumption she would rectify in the future, when her heart didn't shred every time she thought of her baby.

'Mrs Baron will visit you every day, and I'll be back before you know it.'

As if conjured up, their next-door neighbour walked into the ward. The widow, easily fifteen years older than her mother, was nevertheless spry and full of life. Her cheery demeanour was infectious, and her mother was soon chuckling.

An hour later, Suki left the two women chatting, and returned home, thoughts of the email and of Luis darkening her spirits as she opened her front door.

The sight of mail on her doormat roused her from her blanketing sadness. Welcoming the tiny distraction, she walked through to the kitchen.

Two of the three pieces of post were junk mail. The stamp on the third envelope shot her heart into her throat, and her hand was trembling as she ripped the letter open.

Frantically, her gaze flew over the words. Her shocked, tearful gasp echoed through her small hallway. Forcing herself to calm down, she read them again.

You've been accepted...first appointment 15th September...

Folding the paper, she pressed the heels of her hands into her eyes. Seriously, she needed to stop crying. Tears didn't solve problems. Besides, things were beginning to look up. In the last few hours she'd been given a chance to say a proper good-bye to Luis, and granted a once-in-a-lifetime opportunity.

Losing her baby after months of frantically trying to sustain her pregnancy had wrecked her. When the discharge nurse had given her the packet of leaflets the day she'd left hospital, Suki had almost thrown them away. It'd been days before she'd bothered to sift through the brightly coloured pamphlets prescribing various ways to move on from a loss she knew she would never get over.

At first, she'd dismissed the charity offering women in her situation a new alternative. She hadn't planned to get pregnant, nor had she imagined that her one night with Ramon would result in such a staggering roller coaster of joy and turmoil.

All she'd craved was solitude to mourn her lost child and lick her wounds. But those wounds had grown larger every day, with the hole in her heart widening until she feared it would swallow her whole. When she woke up one morning clutching the leaflet, she chose to believe the same fate that had ripped her child from her was offering her a way to heal. Her child would never draw breath, but she had more of the joy she'd felt for that child to give to another.

She hadn't planned on motherhood the first time round. But this time, she would do things her way, without the fear of a man who wouldn't stick around, as her own mother had experienced from her father, or, even worse, infidelity from someone she opened her heart to.

It had been a long shot because the charity accepted only twenty-five non-paying cases a year, so, although she'd secretly hoped, she'd been prepared for a rejection.

She opened the letter again, her mouth slowly curving in a whisper of a smile as she absorbed the soul-saving words.

She retrieved her laptop from the dark nook and took it into the kitchen. Fully immersed in the brilliant sunshine, she first answered Ramon's lawyers giving the time and date of her arrival in Havana, then sent an email confirming the appointment at the fertility clinic.

Then with the hopeful smile on her face, Suki flew up the stairs to her room, dragged the suitcase from her closet, and began to pack.

* * *

Havana in early September was a sweltering vision of vibrant colour. The brief rain shower that had engulfed the plane as they came in to land had already disappeared by the time Suki retrieved her suitcase and made her way through Immigration. Travelling first class had been a singularly unique experience, one she would've appreciated even better had the purpose of this trip not weighed so heavily on her heart. She was thankful that for the most part she'd been left alone to grab what sleep she could, which meant she arrived a lot more refreshed than she had on any other previous plane trip.

Spotting her name on a whiteboard held by a sharply suited chauffeur further hammered home the fact that she was in Luis's homeland. That she was about to come face-to-face with Ramon, the man she'd shared a torrid night with only to wake up alone with no inkling as to the devastating trail of consequences of her actions. The man who still had no clue what had happened to her after he'd walked away in the early hours of the morning.

As she often did when thoughts of Ramon surged, she shoved them back into the box labelled *out of bounds.*

She stood by the decisions she'd made regarding

her pregnancy, even the ones involving swearing Luis to secrecy about the fact that she was carrying his brother's child. He hadn't been pleased, but he'd respected her wish to inform Ramon at a time of her own choosing, once she'd come to terms with the new direction her life had taken.

As it turned out, there'd been no need to involve Ramon because fate had had other ideas…

Following the chauffeur who had taken control of her case, Suki emerged into blinding late afternoon sunshine and a cacophony of Spanish and blaring horns.

Outside José Martí International Airport, the iconic brightly painted nineteen fifties' style taxis lined up in rows next to buses and private cars. Sliding on her sunglasses, she hitched her handbag onto her shoulder and summoned a smile as the driver held open the back door of a stretch limo.

Unlike the luxury car she and Ramon had shared that night a lifetime ago, this car was a silver affair, gleaming in the sunlight and catching the eyes of passers-by. Fighting the strange urge to refuse the ride and find her own, she slid into the car. The tinted windows and the bench seats were identical, the scent of leather engulfing her and catapulting memories she didn't want to remember straight to the forefront of her mind.

Except this time she was alone, reliving every single moment of that night. Just as she'd been alone when she'd learned that her baby would most likely not survive.

Resolutely, Suki turned her thoughts outside, looking out of the window as Havana unveiled itself. It was just as Luis had described often and passionately. Most of the buildings were stuck in their pre-Communism era, with many severely dilapidating as a result of a less than thriving economy. But at every corner there were signs of restoration, pride in a rich heritage exhibited in statues, mosaic-tiled squares, a baroque cathedral and even in the graffiti that littered centuries-old buildings tucked between narrow lanes.

The two-line response from Ramon's lawyers to her email had informed her she would be staying at one of the Acosta hotels in the city. Suki wasn't ashamed to admit to her relief when she'd read the email.

She welcomed the chance to arm herself thoroughly for the next meeting with Ramon.

Traffic was light, and the limo slid beneath the porticoed entrance of the hotel a little over half an hour later.

The Acosta Hotel Havana was a stunning ten-storey building holding pride of place on a palm-tree-lined street that dissected modern Havana City from the world-renowned Old Havana. Straddling the best of both worlds, the six-star hotel had been painstakingly converted from a baroque palace, the designers having retained as many of its original breathtaking features as possible.

Inside, a stunning gold-leaf ceiling depicting an intricate map of the world was highlighted by huge, staggeringly beautiful half-century-old crystal chandeliers, while across the potted-palm foyer, several groupings of stylish leather chairs invited guests to sit and enjoy the formidable architecture.

Suki dragged her avidly exploring gaze away long enough to cross gleaming black and white mosaic tiles to the intricately carved wooden reception desk where a petite, dark-haired receptionist smiled in welcome.

'Miss Langston, welcome to Havana. We hope you will enjoy your stay with us.' She waved over a middle-aged man dressed in burgundy and gold monogrammed uniform and handed him the plastic room card. 'This is Pedro, he'll be your personal butler for the duration of your stay. If you need anything else, please let us know.'

She didn't ask how the receptionist knew her by sight. On the few occasions she'd ventured into Luis's world while he'd been alive, she'd quickly realised that the wealthy and powerful led very different lifestyles. One she got a taster of when, upon arrival in the luxury suite, two additional members of staff unpacked her clothes and a light lunch was set out on a sun-drenched private terrace within minutes.

Suki refused the welcome champagne and mostly picked at her grilled seafood salad. The preoccupation of readying herself for the trip to Cuba had briefly suppressed the jangling nerves that the thought of meeting Ramon again awakened.

They clanged harder now, questions she'd resolutely driven out of her thoughts resurging with brutal force. No matter how many times she tried to tell herself what happened that night had been on equal terms, she still couldn't understand why he'd left her without a word. Was that the done thing? Had she misstepped somehow?

Was that why he'd fast-tracked Luis into moving to New York?

But one question burned most of all, one question she knew deep in her heart had informed some of the decisions she'd made regarding her pregnancy.

Why had he lied about no longer being engaged?

Finding out that Ramon was still engaged to Svetlana after their night together had filled her with numbing disbelief, then horror when Luis had confirmed it. The shock and resulting bitterness at being made an accomplice to infidelity had stayed with her for a long time, and even risked her friendship with Luis. Only her confession about her pregnancy and the associated problems with it had brought a much-needed perspective and support from her best friend.

But now those questions, and more, crowded her brain.

Although her butler spoke perfect English, Suki was reluctant to ask him anything about his employer. The fact that Ramon was choosing to deal with her through his lawyers also indicated that he wished to maintain a distance.

That was fine by her. It should make the decision to tell him about the child they'd lost much easier.

Abandoning her meal, she retreated into the cool suite. A quick check of her emails showed another message from Ramon's lawyers, telling her she would be picked up at nine a.m. for the memorial.

Suki spent the rest of the evening laying out her clothes and taking a bath, after which she slid into bed for an early night.

The soft knock on her door came seconds before her phone's alarm went off at eight the next morning. After trying and failing to swallow more than a bite of the scrambled eggs and toast or stop the ever growing butterflies in her stomach, she took a quick shower and donned her simple black dress and heels. Tying her hair in a knot, she picked up her black clutch just as another knock came on her door.

The butler beat her to it. Which was just as well because the sight of Ramon Acosta filling the doorway wasn't one she could've withstood well up close. Because even across the vast distance of the living room, every single particle in her body clenched tight on seeing him.

He prowled into the room, tall and powerful, his strides measured and predatory. Eyes that had never been soft were now even harsher as they mercilessly raked over her. His mouth, still sensual, still unsmiling, had developed a layer of cruelty and, almost impossibly, his shoulders seemed broader, as if they'd had to expand to accommodate the harrowing circumstances thrown at him.

Even though a part of her heart went out to him for the unthinkable loss he'd suffered, Suki was too busy building the foundation of her own self-preservation as the ground beneath her feet tilted crazily.

Many times before and even after the doctors had informed her of the state of her pregnancy, she'd wondered what their child would look like. She'd eventually discovered she was carrying a girl. Imagining a female version of Ramon had been a little harder than a male version, and perhaps a blessing in disguise in the long run, a way the cosmos chose to help her cope.

Because the man dressed from head to toe in bespoke black standing in front of her was every inch as formidable—goodness, even more so—than her imagination had conjured up.

He stopped before her, eyes of chilled green glass fixed on her. 'Are you not going to greet me, Suki?' he asked icily.

Her gut clenched harder at the sound of his voice. Although it was now arctic, she didn't need much prompting to recall it in a different tone. A huskier, headier timbre. A tone she had no business recollecting right now. She bit her tongue against informing him that he'd entered her domain and therefore etiquette dictated he needed to greet her first. There was no use because men like Ramon played by their own rules. And for her own peace of mind, she wanted the next two days to go as smoothly as possible.

Clearing her throat, she strove for an even tone. 'Good morning, Ramon. I... I wasn't expecting to see you.'

'Were you not?' he countered, unforgiving eyes still hooked into her. 'What were you expecting, *exactly*?'

'Well…not you…here…' She stopped, silently cursed the silly stammering she'd thought was far behind her. 'I mean, I was expecting your driver, not you…to come in person.'

'Then I guess you'll just have to suffer the inconvenience of my presence,' he bit out.

His tone raked across her hackles, making her own chin rise. 'It's not an inconvenience, but surely you have better things to do than personally escort me to the memorial?'

'Indeed, there are many demands on my time. But perhaps everything else paled in comparison to my wish to see you. Perhaps I couldn't wait to clap eyes on you again, reassure myself that you're indeed flesh and blood.'

Something about the way he spoke the words stamped cold, hard dread onto her soul. Frantically she searched his gaze, but his face was an inscrutable mask, the only indication of his demeanour the darkening eyes that continued to regard her with unnerving intensity. 'Flesh and blood? As… as opposed to what?' she asked, her voice not as steady as she craved it to be.

His firm lips flattened. 'As opposed to the many

other descriptions whose veracity I will test once the memorial is over. And believe me, Suki, there are many.'

Her hackles rose higher, her breath shortening as ice filled her spine. 'Well, I don't know what that means, but I assure you, I'm made of the same flesh and blood and bone I possessed when you last saw me.'

Cold eyes grew even more remote, his nostrils pinching white before he took a step back. 'Should I find it curious that you neglected to mention your *heart*?'

Her breath strangled. No, her heart wasn't the same. It'd grown into twice its size when she'd found out she was carrying a child. Then it'd been lacerated beyond repair at the harrowing events and the decisions that had led to the loss of her child. Suki was sure that were she to pluck it out of her chest right this moment, she wouldn't recognise the battered organ.

'Since the contents of my heart are none of your business, no, I don't believe it's a matter for discussion.'

He exhaled slowly, his chest expanding then settling as he regarded her. 'For both our sakes, we will set this aside for now. We will go and remember my brother with our best memories. Then after that, we'll talk.'

She recalled the paragraph in the email that had demanded her attendance at a meeting involving Luis's will, and her heart lurched. 'If this is about Luis's will, please know that if there's any contention I'm willing to relinquish whatever it is that involves me.'

One corner of his mouth twitched with a cruel non-smile as he turned and strolled for the door. 'It's about much, much more than that, Suki. But rest easy, you'll find out soon enough.'

Of course, his assurance achieved the opposite effect. The journey to San Augustino Cathedral in Old Havana took a little over ten minutes, but it felt like several lifetimes with the deadly silence at the back of the limo dragging each second to infinity.

Inside the cathedral, life-size pictures of Luis and his parents were set on easels, their sometimes laughing, sometimes serious, always vibrant faces striking a deep well of sadness and grief inside her. Suki wasn't aware she was silently weeping until a white handkerchief was briskly presented to her. The grateful look she sent to Ramon dissolved when she met his stony profile.

The ceremony was over in a little more than an

hour with the two dozen guests lighting candles and saying a final goodbye to lives cut short too soon.

Suki was setting her lit candle back into its cradle when Ramon appeared beside her. Hoping the acrimony she'd sensed in him had receded, she cleared her throat and faced him.

'Thank you for allowing me to be here, and for sending me the ticket. I promise, I'll pay you back as soon as I'm back at work next month.'

His lip curled. 'Such consideration. Tell me, where was that consideration when you decided to get rid of my baby without so much as a text message informing me?'

Her heart lurched to a stop. She felt the blood drain out of her head as she swayed on her feet. Opening her mouth, she strove for words, for anything to explain. But her brain had closed off in utter shock, her whole body drenched in ice-cold dread as he stepped closer, his body throbbing with menace and rage and dark promises of retribution.

'Nothing to say, Suki?' he scythed at her a second before one hand jerked out to imprison her wrist. With a merciless tug, he brought her flush against his body. To anyone watching it would've seemed as if he were comforting her. But he was leaning close, his lips a hair's breadth from her ear as he whispered, 'Don't worry, I have *plenty* to say. And if you think the repaying of an airplane ticket is the only worry you have, then you're seriously deluded.'

CHAPTER FOUR

NOTHING ABOUT HER disturbed him, Ramon assured himself as his driver pulled away from the cathedral and into traffic. Not the prolonged paleness of her frozen face, the ephemeral fragility of the fingers twisting in her lap, the intermittent shudders that racked her body.

She wasn't cold. Or in pain.

No. Not at all.

It was all an act. Suki Langston was nothing but a stone-hearted liar. One he'd had the misfortune of tangling with for one single night. Long before that night, he'd wondered what Luis saw in her, why their so-called friendship had stretched into years.

He'd concluded that his brother had been fooled as concisely as he had. Not only that, Suki had lured Luis into keeping a secret that shouldn't have been his to keep.

In his darker moments, Ramon wasn't sure he would ever be thankful that his brother had finally gone against his vow and told him the truth.

Because what use was it to be told that something you hadn't even known you possessed had already been ripped from your life? What good did it do when it left you with a gaping wound further compounded by deeper losses?

At first he'd been stunned at the news, even doubting Luis. He'd used condoms the three times he'd taken her. Granted that last time in her bed had been a very close call but he hadn't taken complete leave of his senses to forget protection. But he was aware that prophylactics weren't one hundred per cent foolproof. And very quickly he'd accepted the consequences of that mishap.

What he hadn't accepted then and couldn't accept now were the decisions Suki had taken with regard to what belonged to him.

His fist balled, the rage and grief in his chest multiplying a thousandfold.

It was unfortunate that she chose that moment to flick those wide, duplicitous blue eyes at him.

'How…how long have you known?' Her voice was little above a murmur. As if the strength had been bled from her vocal cords. He believed no such thing. Unfortunately, he was well versed in such female tactics, was accustomed to women who often pretended emotional weakness to gain advantage. In his younger days it'd been a mere ir-

ritant if it meant the woman in question ended up
in his bed. With the passage of time, he'd grown
to abhor it. Svetlana had been a master at it. Little
had she known that he'd been onto her games very
early on in their relationship.

'That's what you're concerned about? How long
I was in the dark before I found out the truth?' he
demanded. 'Not how I feel about you getting rid
of my child?'

She paled even further, but he was in no mood to
show mercy. She'd showed him none and dragged
his brother into colluding with her lies. 'I—'

'Are you aware of what you robbed me of? Do
you know that tying Luis into your web of lies
put a strain between us and deprived me of time
with my brother in the months before he died?'
The words ripped fresh wounds on top of barely
healed ones.

A broken sob tore from her. 'Oh, no! Please,
please don't say that.'

White-hot rage and shredding grief scorched him
from the inside. 'Why not? Because it's too *difficult* to hear?'

She bunched a fist against her mouth, her eyes
shining as she stared at him. 'Yes! It is,' she admitted brokenly.

The car drew to a stop at the private heliport. On

the tarmac his aircraft waited to transport them to the easternmost point of the island that was his true home. The rotor blades were already turning, but he wasn't quite done with her. Wouldn't be for a very long time.

'What right had you to ask that of Luis, hmm? What happened that night was between you and I and no one else. The consequences should have been borne by both of us.'

She squeezed her eyes shut and shook her head. 'I know, and I didn't want to…to tell Luis.'

'Why not? Because it was a dirty little secret you wished to dispose of but couldn't quite accomplish on your own?'

'No! My God, no. Stop twisting my words. Ramon, please listen…' Her mouth trembled as she opened her eyes and sucked in a deep breath.

He inhaled a breath that didn't quite replenish his lungs. Right in that moment he felt as if nothing would ever be right again. He'd lost too much, too soon.

'I have the medical bills from the private clinic, the ones you let my brother pay for. I know *exactly* how much it cost to get rid of my child.'

'Oh, my God,' she whispered.

'No. You're out of luck, *cara*. Not even a higher power is going to save you now.'

She stared at him with wide eyes before her gaze flicked past him, and out of the window at their surroundings. Seeing the readying aircraft, she turned back to him.

'Where are we going?'

'To my villa in Cienfuegos. My lawyers are waiting for us there.'

A wave of apprehension washed over her face. 'I thought we were going back to the hotel. Do... do I need to come with you?'

Another emotion sliced through him. 'You don't wish to know what your so-called best friend bequeathed you?'

She hesitated. 'I do, but...'

'You suddenly fear for your safety?' He couldn't help but mock.

Her chest rose and fell in a steadying breath. 'I fear for the mood you're in. I prefer for us to continue this conversation when you're more rational.'

'The only thing that would make me *irrational* is you choosing to remain in this car one moment longer. Get out, Suki.' He jerked his chin towards the door his driver was holding open for her and waited, teeth clenched, as she slowly stepped out.

Grabbing his own handle, he threw the door open, the space suddenly too small to contain the power and might of his volatile emotions.

Striding across the tarmac behind her, he wondered how he would bear to be in close proximity to her during the helicopter ride when everything in him wanted to shake answers out of her. No, not everything. A small, intensely illogical part of him wanted to curl his hand over that delicate nape of hers, stop her in her tracks and demand that she stop shaking. That she stopped being so damned pale and fragile. Demand to know why she was no longer as curvy as she'd once been.

Madre de Dios...

Ramon was half thankful when his driver helped her into the helicopter. The same part watched her scramble to the farthest seat and buckle herself in, her body throwing up *keep off* signs.

Climbing in beside her, he saw to his own belt, then nodded to his pilot.

Despite the state-of-the-art noise-cancelling interior and the headphones with microphones they donned, he chose silence over continuing their conversation. He needed time to collect himself.

Losing control now would be counterproductive. He'd set a specific plan in motion when he'd instructed his lawyers to bring her here. And he would carry those plans through.

They completed the twenty-five-minute air ride

in silence but he noted that she continued to tremble, her fingers twisting one way then another in her lap.

They landed at the purpose-built heliport at the south end of his villa's garden. Emerging to the small gathering of people at the edge of the tarmac, he caught the questions in her eyes although she refrained from speaking.

Ramon addressed them, shook hands, accepted hugs and fought debilitating emotions that bubbled up when heartfelt condolences were offered up. All through it, Suki stood by in silence, her hands clutching her purse in front of her.

Eventually, when the last of the visitors left, he continued towards the house.

'Who were those people?' she asked as she hurried to keep up with him.

His jaw clenched. 'Our neighbours and Luis's childhood friends.'

The shadow that crossed her face could've been real pain. Or a carefully crafted gesture meant to fool him into thinking she had genuine feelings. *Dios*, he'd had it with calculating women. He clawed his fingers through his hair.

He needed a drink. Badly.

But first there were the lawyers to deal with.

Striding across the terrace, he made a beeline for the hallway that led to his study.

Three of his trusted legal team waited, suits sharp and pens poised to carry out the plan he'd formulated. But first he had to sit through listening to his brother's last words to the woman who had cheated him out of something he hadn't even known he craved until it was gone.

He made quick introductions, ignored the curious stares his lawyers cast her way as he sat at his desk and indicated the chair opposite.

She strode forward, her slimmer hips swaying in the simple but stylish black dress.

Ramon found his gaze lingering over her neatly tied caramel-blonde hair, then lower, scrutinising other areas where her body had changed. Her jawline was more pronounced, her cheeks hollower. Her lightly glossed mouth was still full and attention-grabbing, but her waist was even trimmer, its slightness easily spanned by his hands…

Realising what he was doing, he ruthlessly reeled himself in, but not before he caught the lingering gaze of the youngest member of his legal team on her. A sharp look redirected the man's focus to the papers he held.

'We will conduct the meeting in English. Miss

Langston doesn't speak Spanish…' Ramon paused, one eyebrow raised at her '…unless I'm mistaken?'

She shook her head as she sat down, summoned a whisper of a smile. 'Nothing beyond hello and goodbye.'

Neither of which she would be using on him any time soon. They were light years beyond cordial greetings and he had no intention of letting her out of his sight for a very long time.

His chief legal representative opened the folder before him. 'The reason you're here, Miss Langston, is because of the late codicil attached to the personal will Luis had drafted earlier this year.'

Ramon's nape tightened. 'When was this done?'

'In May, four months ago. On the fifteenth to be exact.'

Suki's breath caught, her throat working furiously.

'What?' he demanded, although he suspected he knew the answer.

'It was the day after…' She stopped, firmed her lips.

He didn't need to hear more. He knew it was the day after she'd first checked into the private clinic. The time and dates Luis had told him were seared into his brain. And if for any reason he needed hard proof, the report from his private investigators was locked away in the top drawer of his desk.

He dragged his focus back to his lawyer. 'Carry on.'

'Miss Langston, I believe at the time the codicil was added you were pregnant?' his lawyer asked.

Still tight-lipped, she nodded.

'Well, Luis didn't alter it so the original document stands. In it, your child was to receive a lump sum of money on his or her eighteenth birthday. But in the event of altered circumstances like what subsequently ensued, half of that sum was to go to you but only at his brother's discretion.'

She shook her head, her eyes finding his. 'You won't need to decide whether I should have the money or not. I don't want it.'

The lawyer's eyebrows rose. 'But you haven't heard how much—'

'I don't care how much it is. I don't want it. Feel free to give it away to Luis's favourite charity.'

Fresh anger boiled in Ramon's gut. 'That's how you're choosing to honour his memory? By tossing away his gift so carelessly?'

The eyes that met his were darker than normal. Bruised. Perhaps she cared about his brother to whatever extent her stone heart was capable. But in the end, her caring hadn't been enough. Luis had assured him he'd tried to talk her out of her decision to no avail.

'That money was never meant for me, Ramon, and you know it. It isn't right,' she murmured, her voice husky.

'Whatever my thoughts are on the matter, this was Luis's wish. You will honour it.'

Her mouth firmed. 'Okay, fine. If I choose to accept it, what then? Will you just hand it over?'

He shrugged. 'That will be one of the subjects of our private discussion.'

A tiny flame lit through her eyes, a spark of anger lightening the dark blue depths that seemed even more vivid against the stark black she wore. 'You just wanted me to say yes so you'd make me jump through hoops, didn't you?'

'I'm not in a habit of handing over a quarter of a million pounds on a fickle whim, Suki, so yes, there will be some hoop-jumping.'

She gasped, her gaze swinging from his to his lawyer's. At the man's nod of confirmation of the sum, she subsided back into her chair. 'That's…a lot of money. Why?'

'You were carrying his niece, and Luis was big on family. As his friend, surely you knew that?' he taunted.

The fire dimmed a little, but her chin elevated.

'Yes, I knew.' Her gaze swung to the lawyers. '*If Mr Acosta decides to release the money to me, I would still like to donate it. Can I contact you if I need to?*'

Temper rising, Ramon watched his lawyer nod, his expression softening.

'*Sí*, of course, Miss Langston.'

Suki started to rise, throwing further fuel on Ramon's mood. 'Sit down, we're not done,' he snapped.

Her gaze reverted to him, then back to his lawyer. The older man cleared his throat. 'Luis also left you two works of art to be handed over on whatever birthday followed his passing. I believe your twenty-sixth birthday is coming up.'

She nodded.

The lawyer continued, 'They're commissioned and paid for, but not yet completed. The artist will let us know when it is ready and you will be informed.'

A tiny frown marred her eyebrows. 'I…who's the artist?'

Ramon hid his sizeable bolt of shock. 'I'm guessing that would be me,' he supplied lazily, both irritated and saddened by Luis's meddling. He looked at his lawyer. 'Correct?'

Her head snapped in his direction, her breath

stopping. 'You...why?' she asked for a second time in the space of three minutes.

'Because according to my brother, you *adore* my work. I believe his paraphrased words after a visit to one of my galleries were, "She rhapsodised over your sculptures for a solid hour and needed to be dragged out of the gallery. I think the poor girl deserves a couple of her own." I never thought he'd actually put the thought to deed in his will.'

Her face reddened, her eyes sliding away from his. 'I didn't... Luis liked to exaggerate. I wasn't that taken...'

'Does that mean you're about to refuse this gift, too?' he enquired, the turbulence inside him curiously emerging in a soft whisper.

Her gaze returned to his. Her lips parted. Ramon found himself holding his breath, unsure whether he wished her to accept or refuse.

'You would still do it? Despite...everything?' Her voice was equally soft, but tinged with bewilderment, not the rage burning beneath his skin.

He allowed himself a twisted smile. 'I loved my brother. I believe in honouring his wishes. The question is, do you?'

Her bewilderment intensified, her tongue sneaking out to lick her lower lip. 'Of course, but, Ramon...'

He actively despised the hot little tug to his groin as he followed the action. 'Is that all of it?' he snapped at his lawyers.

They got the hint, straightened their ties and shuffled papers. 'Yes, that's Miss Langston's part of the meeting concluded. When it's decided what to do with the inheritance, we will be on hand to carry out your wishes.' His chief lawyer switched to Spanish, handing over the papers Ramon had requested with a puzzled expression.

Ramon ignored his concerns. Almost overnight, he'd had everything that meant a damn taken from him. His parents and Luis's loss was unavoidable. The steps Suki had taken were deliberate. He would not be swayed from the path he'd chosen.

The moment the lawyers left he returned his gaze to her.

Watched her gather herself with a deep breath, her eyes fixed on the painting on the far wall of his study. A little colour had returned to her cheeks and she seemed better composed. She was no-where as vibrant as she'd been the last time they were together, but she didn't look deathly pale any more.

Which he chose to see as an advantage. For what was to come she would need all her strength. Or perhaps she would acquiesce simply to get her hands on the money she purportedly didn't want. He knew different. She was in severe dire straits financially.

Rising, he rounded his desk. Her head immediately swung to him, her expression growing wary as she tracked his slow stride. Hitching his thigh on the corner of his desk, he sat down.

Silently, he watched her. Waited.

Her tongue darted out to worry her lower lip again. 'Ramon, I think I need to explain a few things—'

'Explanation is necessary when there's a misunderstanding, an omission of facts, or outright *lying*. There is no such misunderstanding or omission here. You got pregnant with my child and chose to keep that fact to yourself. Then took specific steps to get rid of it. Have I *misunderstood* or *omitted* anything?'

She flinched then slowly her gaze narrowed, the fire returning to her eyes. 'No, you haven't. But you're also forgetting one thing.'

'And what's that?' he asked.

'That it was my body and ultimately *my* decision. Not yours.'

The truth in that statement was inescapable. And while the civilised part of him accepted it, the part steeped in deep mourning and inextinguishable anger couldn't swallow it in that moment. 'So I didn't matter at all in this scenario?' he breathed.

Her hand flew to her forehead, rubbing restively over her smooth skin. 'I didn't say that. The trouble is that you seem to think I took the decision lightly, when it was the last thing I did.'

'How would I know? I wasn't there.'

Her hand dropped, her delicate jaw clenching. 'I know! And you can berate me about that all you want. But I can't change the past. I'm... I'm trying to put it behind me.'

That terrible vice around his heart squeezed tighter. 'Well, I'm not ready to put it behind me. And no, you can't change the past. But you can change the future. And you will.'

Her breath expelled in a little rush of apprehension. 'What's that supposed to mean?'

'It means it's time to discuss the next item on the agenda.'

He reached for the bound papers his lawyers had drawn up and tossed them into her lap.

For long seconds, she looked down at them. Then, slowly, she picked them up, scrutinised the pages with a frown. 'What is this?'

'It's an agreement between you and me.'

She leafed through a few more pages. 'I can see that. But for what? It just says it's an agreement for my *services*. I'm an interior designer and you're a hotelier and artist. What service could you possibly want from me?'

'I don't need your professional services, *cara*. What I want is for you to provide me with what you took deliberate steps to deprive me of. My whole family was wiped out in a single night. I want a child, Suki. An heir. As soon as possible. Preferably in the next nine months. And you're going to give me one.'

CHAPTER FIVE

DEEP SHOCK AND confusion held her frozen in the chair for countless seconds. Then Suki surged to her feet. She tossed the papers back onto the desk, unable to get her fingers off them quickly enough.

'Are you out of your mind?' She should've posed the question rhetorically because she was one hundred per cent sure that he had gone insane. From grief or from something else, but definitely unsound.

Except he didn't look crazy. Only brutally determined, eerily controlled. 'Far from it,' he confirmed. 'In fact, this is probably one of the sanest decisions I've ever made.'

Her already racing heart tripped over itself to speed up even more. 'Then I'm terrified to imagine what you class as sane!'

A cold smile curved his mouth. 'Let's concentrate on one item at a time.'

'We will not concentrate on any items because what you're...*suggesting* isn't going to happen,' she returned. She didn't realise she was backing away from the chair, from him, until he rose to his imposing height and prowled after her.

'Where do you think you're going?'

'Where do you think? I'm leaving!'

'No. You are not.' His voice was deadly soft.

Goose bumps rose on her skin but she kept moving away. 'Watch me.'

'I am watching you. And I don't think you realise how very little options you have here.'

'I have the option of *not* staying here to continue this insane conversation with you.'

His hands slid lazily into his pockets, but there was nothing indolent in the eyes that tracked her backward trajectory with narrow-eyed intensity. 'You can leave this room, but how do you propose to make your escape from this house?'

Her back touched the study door and she froze. 'You… I seriously hope you're not suggesting that you intend to keep me here against my will!'

'That entirely depends on you. You can walk out of here and attempt to make the three-hour journey back to Havana on your own or we can finish this conversation.'

She shook her head, knowing deep inside that things weren't that simple. The alarming suspicion that he'd planned all this with meticulous precision grew with each second he stared at her.

'I'll make the journey on my own, thank you.'

She needed to get out of here. The trip back would be costly, but she'd stick it on her credit card and think about the consequences later.

Reaching behind her, she grasped the handle, turned it. Relief flooded her when it yielded. It occurred to her that once she turned and walked away, this would probably be the very last time she set eyes on Ramon. A tiny second was all she needed to take in the sculpted beauty of his face, the square designer-stubble jaw, the impossibly wide shoulders that Luis had once told her had been honed from his days playing quarterback at college in the States, the lean, hard-packed body that stretched over pure, streamlined muscle.

She took all of it in, stored it in a file somewhere deep in her subconscious, unwilling to admit that some time in the future she would revisit it. Just as she'd revisited their night together more times than she felt comfortable admitting even to herself.

Pulling the door wider, she stepped through it. 'Goodbye, Ramon.'

'Is your hurry to get back to do with your appointment with the sperm donor agency or your mother?' he enquired in an almost indifferent voice.

Suki turned back so swiftly she almost tripped over her feet. The way he leaned so casually against the doorjamb, legs crossed at the ankles, made her believe she'd misheard him. Because surely he wouldn't look that bored while informing her he'd callously invaded her privacy. *'What did you say?'*

He remained silent, those all-knowing green eyes pinned on her.

'Did you not hear me? I said—'

'I heard you, and you know exactly what I said. I just prefer not to conduct this conversation in the hallway in the hearing of my staff, especially if you insist on using that shrill voice.'

Suki swallowed down the scream that rose; squashed the urge to march up to him, take him by his expensive designer lapels and shake the living daylights out of him. It would be useless because she suspected he would remain just as unmoved as he seemed now.

She shook her head in abject confusion. 'What gives you the right to invade my privacy?'

'You don't seem to have grasped the reality before you, Suki.' He stepped back from the door, his hands leaving his pockets to hang almost menacingly against his masculine thighs. 'So come back in and let's discuss this rationally. Now,' he added after a handful of seconds when she remained frozen.

'All this…the ticket, the hotel, coming here to meet with your lawyers…it was all one giant plan, wasn't it?'

'*Sí*, it was,' he confirmed, not a trace of apology in his face or voice. 'Oh, and I forgot to mention. Your things were moved here from the hotel while we were at the memorial. So bear that in mind if you decide to make another grand exit.'

Her mind sped with the thinly veiled threat in his voice.

Her things…including her passport and airline ticket. 'Oh, God. You…'

'Need your undivided attention *without* the histrionics.'

The reality of what was happening rammed home in that instant. She could try to leave but she wouldn't get very far. So really, she was going nowhere until he deemed it so.

On leaden legs, she returned to the study. The sound of the door shutting felt like the slam of prison gates.

She tightened her fingers around her clutch to

stop their trembling. 'I can report you to the authorities. You know that, right?'

He raised a mocking eyebrow. 'For having a simple conversation with a guest after my brother's memorial?'

'There's nothing simple or remotely funny about this, and you know it,' she replied heatedly.

All traces of mockery evaporated from his face, leaving a harsh, bleak mask. 'On that we're agreed,' he bit out. One hand rose to spear agitated fingers through his hair. 'Did you stop to think that, had I been in the picture, things could've turned out differently?'

Suki didn't want to admit that the thought had crossed her mind when the doctors had first given her the diagnosis. But in those initial harrowing weeks, she'd clung vainly to hope. Then the tabloids' timely confirmation of Ramon and Svetlana's still very much *on* engagement had usefully reiterated why any reliance on the man who'd slept with her while still committed to another woman, who'd proven most categorically that he was untrustworthy, was out of the question. Father of her child or not, the knowledge that she couldn't trust Ramon with so momentous a decision had kept her silent. 'How?' she asked, despite knowing they wouldn't have been.

'For a start, had you come to me, you would be in a financially better place now than you currently are.'

She frowned. 'Financially better place? What are you talking about?'

'Luis helped you with your medical bills, did he not? Did you stop to think that going ahead with the pregnancy, that presenting me with my child, would have made you rich beyond your wildest dreams?'

She staggered, actually staggered back at the accusation. 'Are you telling me you think I deliberately got rid of the baby because it wasn't *financially viable*?'

'I had my investigators look into your financial history, Suki. I know you're broke.'

She struggled to take a breath. 'I understand that we were little more than strangers. And we didn't even like each other very much,' she ventured. 'But I would never...never dream of—'

'Drop the excuses, Suki. Nothing you say will excuse your actions. Having my child was an inconvenience you took care of without bothering to tell me,' he cut across her, jaw clenched into stone. Turning, he headed back to his desk and picked up two files and the bundle of papers she'd discarded minutes ago and strode towards her, savage purpose in every step.

He casually opened the file he held. Suki recognised the charity's logo on the letterhead immediately. 'Which begs the question, why would you get rid of my child, then make yourself a charity case for a sperm donation four months later?' There was something dangerously deadly in his voice. A scalpel-sharp control that said he was stroking the very edge of his endurance.

She swallowed, knowing instinctively that the *none of your business* line was the last thing she wanted to throw at him right now. A tremble shivered down her spine. Retreating until she had the grouping of studded leather sofas and a coffee table between them, she attempted to reason with him. 'Ramon, the past is the past. This thing…what you're suggesting…it doesn't make sense.'

His harsh exhalation stopped her stuttering. He glanced up, eyes like the frozen wastelands of Siberia blasting her. 'Why, Suki? Why, for some unconscionable reason, have you decided you want a child now?'

She raised her chin. 'I don't have to explain myself to you.'

A thousand expressions flitted through his eyes, not a single one of them decipherable. Slowly, he shut the file and, without taking his eyes off her, tossed it on the coffee table.

'Okay. Let's talk about something else. Your mother is currently in a private hospital with health complications triggered by stage two cervical cancer, yes?' he pressed.

Her heart lurched painfully. 'Yes,' she murmured.

'With her insurance about to run out this month and her doctors all set to throw in the towel, nothing short of a miracle will bring any hope.' There was no malice in his voice, but neither was there any warmth or sympathy. For reasons she knew were coming, he was laying out the facts of her life in bare chunks.

A spike of anger tunnelled through her bewildered emotions. 'And let me guess, you suddenly have the power to grant miracles?'

'I have more than that. I have the financial power that fuels *particular* miracles. I'm also trying to discover what your goals are. Is this baby you're hoping to have a means of alleviating future loss? Having decided that you didn't want a child before, you're now desperate for one so should your mother not make it you won't be left alone?' he demanded chillingly.

'I don't know what kind of monster you think I am, but what you're suggesting is detestable.'

'Is it?' he enquired, his tone a touch softer, a touch more...vulnerable.

Her eyes widened as what he'd said before made clearer meaning. 'That's why *you* want a child? So you're not alone?'

Pain flickered over his face. 'I want a family, yes,' he confirmed.

'And digging up my mother's records, what does that achieve except to make me think you're leveraging my mother's health against me?'

'It's not leverage. It's an offer of help so, when we reach agreement, you have one less thing to worry about. Those miracles you scoffed about can happen.'

She laughed. She couldn't help herself. 'You actually expect me to believe that you'd do that out of the goodness of your heart, after going to this trouble to bring me here?'

He didn't answer for a long minute. When he did, his voice was bleak. 'For some reason Luis held both you and your mother in high regard, and yet you were prepared to walk away from the inheritance he left you just to make a point when that money could've helped your mother. Luis isn't around any more to make you see sense. But I am.'

She shook her head. 'That money was meant for the child I never had.'

'It was meant for you. But like everything else, you threw it away without a second thought. You think Luis just *overlooked* the fact that you were no longer pregnant when he chose not to amend his will? He knew your mother was ill. Did you not think this might be his way of helping you?'

'I don't know. I had no idea what he was thinking—'

'Perhaps this! What is happening here right now. Maybe he rightly believed that you owe me answers. That *you owe me*, full stop.' His fist was bunched, his nostrils pinched in a tight leash on his control.

She refused to back down. 'Regardless of that, I don't deserve that money.'

'Does your mother deserve your abandonment?'

'I haven't abandoned her! I've done everything I can for her—'

'Have you? Or did you make the barest minimum effort then stop, just like you did with our child?'

Fresh whips lashed her heart. 'You have no right to say that to me—'

'I have every right. And more. For what you did there is no coming back. Only reparations.'

'I'm sorry I didn't tell you the moment I found out! Is that what you want to hear? Do you want me to get down on my knees and beg your for-giveness?'

'You know what I want.'

She flung her clutch on the sofa, every cell in her body too agitated to contain her. 'How can you even propose something like this...how can you contemplate doing something so *life-changing* when you stare at me with such hate? And have you even paused for a second to think about *my* feelings?'

He swivelled towards the window, his features carefully schooled as he raked a hand through his hair. For a long time, she thought he wouldn't an-swer her questions. When he turned back, his fea-tures were set even harder, his eyes completely inscrutable.

'I don't need to like you to take you to bed,' he replied. While she was grappling with that, he added, 'And vice versa. I believe right before our last connection we were less than impressed with each other. Yet, we still proved that we were com-patible where it counted.'

Her senses reeled with the enormity of his rea-soning. 'You think that tipsy interlude compares in any way to this...*clinical* exercise you're pro-posing?'

'Yes, I do. And this time we're going into this

with clear minds and a finite purpose. And you mistake me by thinking this is something you can argue away.'

'And you do likewise by thinking this is something you can force on me. My answer is no.'

'There won't be any force involved. You'll stay here, take the night to sleep on it. Come morning, you will give me an answer. And I prefer that answer to be yes.'

'Or what?'

'Or nothing. And by nothing I mean we will both walk away empty-handed. You will not be returning to England to get yourself impregnated by some faceless sperm donor. I suggested that your place be given away to another needful applicant as of this morning.'

She gasped. *'What?'*

'You're not deaf. On top of that, I have personally put in place a facility for an additional fifty women to receive similar funding. The charity is beyond thrilled. They won't take your name off the list without your express confirmation, but I dare say you're no longer at the top of their list. Not once I informed them that you'd be giving the traditional way another try with me.'

The ground shook beneath her feet. 'You...you can't do that!'

He nodded to the discarded file. 'You underestimate how much I want this, Suki. You're still on the waiting list with the charity, but if you truly wish to get pregnant any time soon, I'm your only option.'

'That's…that's blackmail.'

'You'll be good enough not to fling disparaging labels around, *cara*. What you did was far worse.'

The urge to scream again rose. She barely managed to keep it together to raise her hands in a placatory gesture when she wanted to find the nearest letter opener and stick it in his black heart. 'Ramon. Please hear me out. What I did…my decision… I didn't think I had a choice…' Her voice broke. Swallowing, she shook her head. 'I didn't have a choice…' she repeated.

Ramon's face paled, his features slackening for a brutal, painful moment, before it clenched back into a tight, furious mask. The eyes that stared back at her were almost black with volcanic rage. 'You had a choice. Me. But you were too selfish to bring me into the equation. You made the decision on your own.'

'My God, you accuse me of so many things, but what about you?'

His brows clamped tight. 'What about me?'

'You told me you were no longer engaged, and yet weeks later I found out it was a lie!'

His jaw flexed for a second. 'And that is the reason you called my brother when you should've called me? That is why you handed him the responsibility when it should've been mine to bear?'

Her breath shuddered out. 'I didn't hand anyone the responsibility. I didn't call Luis. My mother did.'

He stilled, straight eyebrows clenched tighter in a dark frown. 'Your mother?'

She nodded, her head barely able to perform the movement. 'She was home from hospital but weak from her chemo. She knew what was going on and she felt bad that she couldn't help me. I told her I didn't need help but she...she wouldn't listen. She thought she was letting me down. She knew Luis and I were close friends but she assumed our relationship had grown into something more. Anyway, she assumed he was the father and called him. Apparently, she had a long go at him for shirking his responsibilities. Luis didn't say a word to refute the claim. He just...turned up at my house the next day and refused to leave.'

'And let me guess. That was when you swore him to secrecy to keep me from my own child?' His voice bled fire and ice.

'I was going to tell you. I didn't think you would appreciate hearing it from him. And I thought I had time. But then things just...unravelled.'

He breathed in a harsh breath. 'You say that and yet you found time to call on Luis a second time to hold your hand through the procedure.'

It staggered her how much detail he knew. And how things looked from his side of the fence. 'I didn't ask him to come, Ramon. But he wasn't prepared to take no for an answer.'

He gave an arid laugh. 'You found it so easy to give in to him, the same way you found it easy to make up excuses not to contact me.'

'How dare you—?'

His hand slammed on the desk, making her jump. 'I dare because I am without my child, and you're to blame!'

Pain shook her from scalp to toes. 'You preach at me from your lofty pedestal about doing the right thing. Did you stop to think that after lying to me about Svetlana that I'd want nothing to do with you? Or are you going to tell me that those pictures in the papers of the two of you taken in the weeks after we were together were your doppelgängers?'

His jaw worked for a long moment before he exhaled. 'What happened between you and I was a one-night thing. If memory serves it was what you wanted, what we both wanted.'

The fact that he was justifying his actions shouldn't have come as a surprise. Wasn't that how she had come into this world? Hadn't she heard a version of the same story from her mother about her father's justification for his infidelity? The only difference here was that Ramon had apparently wanted the seed he'd unwittingly planted in her womb. Suki's father hadn't even stuck around for the pregnancy test announcing she was on the way.

The end result of that had been a mother steeped in so much bitterness she'd never trusted another man long enough to move on from the past. From a very early age, Suki had vowed to learn from that lesson, until she'd met Luis and had eventually chosen to hope that all men weren't the same.

Luis had been one in a million, and she'd trusted him with her life. Unfortunately, she'd been foolish enough to transfer some of that faith to his older brother.

She didn't plan on making the same mistake again.

Refocusing on Ramon, she shook her head. 'There's no way this can ever work. Too much has happened. Besides, what about Svetlana? Won't she have a huge say in what you're proposing?'

'She and I have been over for several months.' The words were clipped. Final.

Suki told herself the fluttering in her stomach was a side effect of the strain of the conversation. 'The same kind of *over* you meant the last time?'

His eyes gleamed, his focus unwavering. 'The kind of over that means she has no bearing on this conversation.'

She wanted to press for more. Why, she had no idea. Whether Ramon and Svetlana were over or not had no impact on her life. There were more important things to focus on, like the reason he had a file on her mother.

'Did you know about Luis's financial bequest before today?'

'No, but he was fond of you. It doesn't surprise me he would take such an action.'

Her head still reeled from that. 'I don't know what to say...'

Another bleak expression darted across his face. 'If he were here right now, what do you think he'd say with regard to your mother's condition?'

Suki's heart twisted, her best friend's vibrant face rearing up vividly in her mind's eye. 'He would help me beg, borrow or steal to help her.'

'*Sí*, he would. And what do you think he would say to you helping me to continue his family line?' he countered smoothly.

She gasped at the skilful way he'd cornered her. 'That's not fair.'

'Is it not, or are you being a hypocrite? He's left you a means to help your mother. Should her treatment exceed what he left for you, I'll pick up the slack.' He paused, his eyes still fixed on her. 'Are you going to let pride and stubbornness stand in the way of your mother's health?'

'No, of course not! But I can't help but think this is…a cold transaction.'

'It's a transaction where we both win.'

Her heart shuddered. 'But her doctors say there's nothing else they can do.'

'They were wrong.' Returning to the sofa, he picked up the last file and handed it to her.

Hands shaking, she opened it, started to read. The names that jumped out at her were from some of the best teaching hospitals and medical research facilities in the world. She recognised them because she'd come across several of them in her own research. Letters from acclaimed doctors with countless abbreviations after their names had personally answered all of the pertinent questions Ramon had posed them. Without offering guarantees, at least half a dozen different doctors had given her mother far better odds than her current doctors had.

'Everything in there has been double and triple checked. All that's required for your mother to get the help she vitally needs is to say yes.'

Suki closed her eyes, three unshakeable truths becoming crystal clear. Her mother's case wasn't hopeless. Luis, in his own inimitable way, was caring for her even from the grave. But by doing so, he'd also put her directly in his brother's debt.

And there was only one means by which Ramon Acosta wanted payment.

CHAPTER SIX

SHE WENT THROUGH the paperwork, noting the recommendation for her mother's treatment to be started immediately, preferably at a state-of-the-art facility in Miami. Closing the file, Suki walked to the sofa and sat down.

The pressure that had been building since Ramon walked into her hotel room this morning intensified. Her pulse raced and in a fit of agitation she reached up and tugged the pins from her hair. The simple of act of unknotting her hair brought a tiny bit of relief. But her mind continued to spin at the sheer enormity of what he was asking of her.

Spiking her fingers into her hair, she briefly massaged her scalp, then raised her head to the dominating figure poised like a dark overlord before her. His gaze was on the heavy tresses gliding over her hands and down her shoulders. He seemed momentarily fascinated with what she was doing, but, too soon, dark unwavering green eyes locked on hers once more.

'Are you ready to discuss this properly?'

She took a deep breath. 'You can have any woman you want. You only have to click your fingers to have them lining up outside your gate to have your baby. Why go to these lengths? And why me?'

This time the trace of pain was fleeting, very hurriedly controlled. 'I can't just pluck a surrogate off the Internet. These things take months, sometimes even years to find a right match.'

'What about your little black book? Surely you have conquests that went beyond a one-night stand, who will be happy to bear you a child?'

His full lips compressed. 'I haven't yet come across a woman who, no matter how much she initially claims otherwise, doesn't start imagining a deeper, more meaningful relationship with me at some point. I'm not interested in that.'

'Right. You were so not interested in that that you were once engaged to be married?'

He ignored her sarcasm. 'I was once engaged because I believed a relationship was a viable option for me. I no longer believe that. Marriage is not for me. And why you?' He shrugged. 'Because you require a sperm donor and I happen to need a surrogate. The timing couldn't be better. Besides, with you I know exactly what I'm getting.'

'And what's that?'

'A black-and-white transaction with no frills, no insincere platitudes and one hundred per cent commitment signed in ink.'

Her chest squeezed tight. 'I'm not just going to hand over my baby to you the moment he or she is born, Ramon. You can forget that right now.'

Two things happened right then. All six feet four inches of him froze in rigid attention. And Suki realised just what she'd said.

'So you agree to bear my child?' he clipped out after a long moment, his voice strangely hoarse.

Her breath shook out. 'I…no. Not yet.'

'This is very much a yes or no situation.'

'And I very much would like five minutes to think about what I'm agreeing to before I say yes to bringing another child into this world!'

He rocked back on his heels, then turned towards his desk. 'While you think about it, I'll get the kitchen to bring you some refreshments.'

Her raw laugh scraped her throat. 'Canapés aren't going to make deciding any easier.'

'Neither will starvation and dehydration. You're much thinner than you were the last time I saw you.'

'Yes, I've been through a trauma or two,' she replied.

'I'm aware of that. But we still need to remedy that,' he countered.

'Fine, let's fatten me up for the slaughter,' she muttered under her breath, because he was already lifting the phone, relating instructions in rapid Spanish.

That done, he returned to his position as silent, merciless master in front of her. After several minutes had gone by, he crossed over and sat down next to her. Elbows on his knees, he angled his body towards hers.

'What is it, Suki? Spit it out.'

She didn't want to say the words out loud, but the fear in her heart wouldn't dissipate. 'I'm…are you not afraid that something will go wrong?' *Again.*

A muscle ticced in his jaw. 'You were about to get yourself artificially inseminated. What guarantees do you have that that pregnancy will proceed smoothly?'

Her heart twisted. 'None.'

He nodded. '*Muy bien.* Then we are in the same boat. But rest assured we will have the benefit of the top obstetricians in the world monitoring you round the clock.'

The assurance eased the constriction around her heart, followed swiftly by the realisation that she was seriously contemplating agreeing to Ramon's wishes.

'What do you think he would say to you helping me to continue his family line?'

Her heart tugged painfully, the belief that Luis would've urged her on so strong, her breath caught. Whether that was the reason the constriction further eased in her chest, or because she now had fresh hope for her mother, she didn't know. And even if she seriously considered refusing, with Ramon determined to throw himself in the way of her having a child any other way but with him, her options for a child of her own were limited, considering she had very little financial resources left.

But another child...with Ramon? Her insides clenched with apprehension at the thought of creating another child, this time deliberately with him. But next to that apprehension, a tiny quiver she refused to label as hope and excitement began to unfurl. She pushed it back down, unwilling to let it spring forth when there was so much more to consider.

'How will we manage this? You work and travel all over the world. I live in England. You know I'm not about to hand over my child to you the moment it's born. So how is this going to work?'

'Our child will be born here in Cuba. Once he or

she is old enough, relocating my offices anywhere in the world will not be a problem. We will decide when the time comes how that will be handled.'

She frowned. 'I have a job, Ramon. You expect me to what...just give it up to sit around while waiting to have your baby?'

'I would prefer that you do not work while you're pregnant and of course in the first few years of the baby's life—'

Her stunned laughter stopped him. 'You're joking, aren't you? That's not how the real world works. I have bills to pay, my mother to look after once her treatment is over.'

'How do you intend to do that when your latest request to return to work was denied?'

Her mouth dropped open. 'Is there any part of my life that you haven't dug up yet?'

'I don't know what your favourite colour is or which brand of toothpaste you prefer. But we have time for that.' He picked up the agreement and held it out to her. 'Read the agreement, a little more carefully this time. Pay attention to clause five.'

She eyed him for a few seconds before she accepted the papers. The clause he mentioned was on the third page. Shock bolted through her, blurring her vision after she'd counted six zeros. 'You can't...this is another joke, right?'

'This is to ensure that our child remains your number one priority. To ensure you don't have to think about bills or work or anything beyond our baby's welfare. Your mother too will be well taken care of.'

'I hadn't planned on anything else superseding my child's well-being but...this is an absurd amount of money.'

His sensual mouth pursed. 'You seem to have trouble grasping that nothing about this discussion is humorous, Suki.'

'Probably because I'm still finding it hard to believe that you truly want this.'

He grabbed the papers from her and once again shoved them aside. His hands cupped her shoulders, bringing her close enough so she didn't miss every flicker of emotion that crossed his face.

'I want a child, Suki. You will be the woman who bears me that child. Is there some other way you wish me to say that before you believe that I mean it?' he rasped in a deep, fervid voice.

Perhaps it was the electric burn of his hands on her bare skin. Or the minute tremble in his voice that spoke of soul-deep intent and yearning. Whatever it was, it cut through the fog of her remaining indecision. Even before her head had fully grasped her intent, her heart had accepted that this was what she would do.

For her mother.

For herself.

Perhaps most of all for Luis. The knowledge that she would play a hand in ensuring her friend's bloodline lived on filled her with the same sense of joy she'd been honoured to receive from Luis. Through her child, she would always have a piece of her friend.

'No, you don't need to say anything else,' she whispered.

'So you agree?'

She nodded again. 'Yes.'

He stared down at her for another long spell, his thumbs absently sliding back and forth on her skin before his gaze dropped to her lips. As if he'd touched them, they tingled wildly, the blood plumping them until she slicked her tongue over her lower lip to alleviate the sting.

'What time frame do we have to work with?'

She frowned. 'I…what?'

'Is the window closing on this month's cycle?' he demanded.

That wasn't a question she'd expected. Because those weren't questions near strangers asked each other.

She closed her eyes as heat flared up her face. 'I… I'm… God, I can't believe I'm discussing my menstrual cycle with you.'

'It's a naturally occurring event and nothing to be embarrassed about,' he replied.

'I'm not embarrassed, I'm just…'

'Being very English about it?' he enquired with a dry tone. 'Would you have preferred us to discuss the weather first before we got to the nitty-gritty?'

She shrugged. 'Maybe. There's absolutely nothing wrong with discussing the weather.'

One side of his mouth quirked. 'Maybe I will oblige you next time,' he answered. Then waited.

'Yes, I stop ovulating in three days,' she eventually murmured.

His gaze dropped back to her mouth, his nostrils flaring lightly as he leaned closer, filled her personal space with his larger-than-life aura. 'Then you will come to me tonight.'

Too soon. Much too soon. Suki swallowed. 'No.'

He stilled. *'Perdón?'*

She shook her head. 'I said no. Not tonight. I just… I need a little time to take all of this in.'

A frown gathered at his forehead. 'Nothing will change with more time,' he warned.

'I know that, but I'm still taking the time I need.'

His mouth pursed into a forbidding line. But any

response coming her way was halted by the knock on the door. A handful of seconds passed before he released her. At his command, a member of his kitchen staff entered wheeling a serving trolley piled with trays of hot and cold beverages, pastries and neatly cut sandwiches.

The middle-aged woman smiled affectionately at Ramon before setting the tray on the coffee table. 'This is Teresa. She's my housekeeper.' He repeated the other side of introduction in Spanish, to which Teresa smiled and responded, adding a few more words Suki didn't understand.

Ramon shook his head and dismissed her, then reached out to place several pieces of pastry on a plate. Passing it to her, he indicated the drinks. 'Which would you prefer?'

She wanted to laugh at the mundaneness of eating following the tense last hour.

'Coffee, please. Thanks.'

He poured two cups, adding sugar and cream to hers at her request before passing it over.

For a few minutes he drank his coffee without making conversation while she nibbled on a finger sandwich. Unable to stand the tension, she picked up another triangle of pastry, and bit into it. The unexpected flavoursome guava and cream cheese filling made her mouth water, her very empty stomach reminding her how long it'd been since she last ate.

'What are these?' she asked, more to make conversation than anything else.

'They're called *pastelitos*. Teresa makes the best ones.' He nudged the tray towards her. 'Have another one.'

She didn't refuse. A barest trace of amusement whispered over his face as he watched her devour a second one.

'After we finish eating, I will show you to your suite. When you're rested, I'll introduce you to the rest of the staff and give you a tour of the villa.'

Grateful for the first normal conversation she'd had since he'd turned up at her hotel this morning, she took another bite. 'Thanks, that would be good.'

'Tomorrow morning, Suki. I will not wait longer than that.'

The thought of him and her...in broad daylight... threatened to send the *pastelitos* and coffee down the wrong way. 'Tomorrow *night*,' she countered quickly after swallowing.

He didn't frown, but the air of displeasure once again shrouded him as he set his cup back onto the saucer. 'Any reason why you wish to waste a further twenty-four hours?'

She tried a shrug, but it didn't quite come off as smoothly as she would've wished. 'Isn't it enough that we've agreed to do this thing? Is there any reason why we need to...umm do it during the *day*?'

The slight widening of his eyes was the only indication that he was surprised. That surprise turned swiftly into sardonic amusement. 'Are you trying to tell me that you only engage in sex at night, Suki?' he drawled.

She set her cup and saucer on the table. 'We've discussed my monthly cycle. There is no way I'm discussing my sexual history with you.'

'How many lovers have you had?' he asked in the next breath.

'Perhaps you didn't hear me—'

'I heard you. Answer my question.'

She stared back at him, the need to challenge burning inside her. 'You go first,' she said, knowing it would put an end to the absurd line of questioning.

He gave her a number. A number much lower than she'd anticipated. 'Close your mouth, Suki. Not everything you read in the papers is accurate. In fact I'll stake my fortune on the fact that ninety per cent of what's said about me is false. Now, it's your turn.'

She closed her mouth, knowing the number she

was about to reveal would scream her woeful inexperience. 'Two,' she muttered.

An expression sparked through his eyes, gone far too quickly for her to decode. 'Two?' he pressed.

'Yes.'

When he continued to regard her with probing eyes, she dropped her gaze. He caught her chin, redirected her gaze to his. '*Including* me?'

She jerked out a nod, then pulled away. She was a touch surprised when he released her. 'Including you.'

'Was the other a long-term boyfriend?' he demanded.

Dear God…

'No, a *very* brief, very much regretted one-time thing that was over almost before it started.' Setting back her empty plate, she stood. 'There, are we done with the questions? Can I go now?'

He rose beside her, immediately towering over her. Even in her heels, she didn't come up to his shoulders. Recalling how overwhelmed she'd been, how much more fragile being in his arms had felt that night when she'd invited him to her bedroom, she took a hasty step back.

He saw the action and his lips thinned.

Scattered around them were the papers and files of her life, reminders of the reason Ramon Acosta had brought her here. Reminders of what she'd agreed to do. The apprehension that hadn't quite died rose again.

'If you're thinking of changing your mind about this, you're wasting your time,' he warned softly, accurately reading her thoughts.

She sucked in a breath. The tiny wisps of amusement that had briefly lightened their simple meal were gone.

'I gave you my word, Ramon. And I meant it. I know what's at stake here.'

Dark satisfaction glinted in his eyes, giving her a glimpse of the ruthless streak that had made him the powerful man he was today. He'd done his homework, searched out her weak points and presented her with an unbreakable deal.

He waited until she'd retrieved her bag before he led her from the study.

The multi-arched hallway leading to the giant entry turned out to be one of several. Even while her mind grappled with her current situation, the interior designer in her was bowled over by the stunning architecture of Ramon's villa.

Large swathes of baroque had been blended with surprising Moorish designs that should have been out of place here, but oddly complemented the building. Along the upper parts of the walls and windows, over two dozen shades of stained glass let in multi-coloured light. Suki wasn't aware her steps had slowed to a halt until he retraced his back to her.

She'd been too distracted to take in more than a glimpse of the majestic stonemasonry of the villa from the outside, but now she was up close, she couldn't resist, reaching out to trace her hand over salmon-coloured carvings set into the nearest arch. 'How old is this place?'

'The original building is fifteenth century. It's been altered a few times since then, hence the eclectic nature of the architecture,' he replied.

She nodded. Wanted to ask more. But she wasn't here for a guided tour into the past.

No. Her presence here was all about the future. Advancing the progeny of the Acosta family.

Her hand dropped from the wall, her senses lurching in wild alarm again at the enormous responsibility she'd undertaken. With a touch of desperation, she pushed it to the back of her mind.

She wouldn't think about it right now. She had more immediate hurdles to overcome. Like informing her mother of what she'd agreed to on her behalf. Like dealing with her boss.

The latter could wait a few more days. Her mother couldn't.

She turned from the wall to find him watching her. 'What is it?'

'I need to call my mother, let her know what's happening.'

He weighed the request for a moment before he nodded. 'There's a phone in your suite you can use. Come.'

He led her through two more hallways, passing an inner courtyard complete with iron trellis, balconies and mosaic fountain before they reached a grand central staircase leading to the upper floors. Ramon turned right at the top of the stairs, past several doors to the last but one set of double doors at the end of the corridor.

Throwing it open, he took a few steps in and stopped. 'You should find everything you need in here. Teresa doesn't speak much English but the younger members of staff do. Dial zero on the phone if you require anything else. I'll ensure one of them is on hand to answer your call.'

'Are you...will you not be around?' she asked.

'I have a few things to attend to in Havana. I'll be back tonight.'

The part of her that had conjured him up as her permanent shadow until she was successfully impregnated didn't know what to do with the fact that he was leaving, albeit only for a few hours.

'Right…okay.'

They stared at one another for an age, the silence between them still fully charged. But after the torrent of words they'd exchanged, there seemed to be nothing more to say. Except there was something else that needed to be answered.

'Umm, what happens after…after I get pregnant?'

'You mean, will I still want to share your bed?'

She jerked out a nod.

His gaze swept down for a spell before it reconnected with hers. 'Once you're pregnant, there won't be any need to have sex.'

A sensation rolled through her she had a hard time defining. But she nodded briskly. 'Good. Great.'

His gaze eventually swung past her, looked around the room, his thoughts completely turned off to her. But Suki caught that look of bleakness she'd spotted intermittently through the day. As he turned towards the door, his profile highlighted that expression even further.

'Wait,' she said before she could stop herself.

He stopped, looked over his shoulder. 'What is it?' There was a hint of weariness. And a lot of wariness.

Her fingers twisted the strap of her handbag.

'You never answered my emails. I guess I know why now. But in case you didn't get round to reading them, I think you need to know what I said in all of them. I'm very sorry for your loss. Luis was a very special person. I'm sure your parents were too.'

He stood stock-still, his face tightening for an infinitesimal second. Then he gave a curt nod. *'Muchas gracias,'* he murmured softly.

A second later he was gone. And she was left in the middle of the most incredible suite she'd ever seen.

The small living room was decorated in tones of cream and burgundy. Heavy drapes were counterbalanced with white muslin curtains that fluttered in the light breeze from the open shuttered windows. Beneath her feet, luxurious cream carpeting muffled her footsteps as she walked to the light-coloured sofas facing each other in front of a small stone fireplace.

The fireplace itself was an exquisitely carved masterpiece, another testament to the skill and dedication that had gone into the villa's design. Setting her bag down on the low wooden coffee table, she walked through another set of doors.

The four-poster queen-sized bed was an eye-catching work of art of wood and iron and expensive linens that made the interior designer in her stop and stare and sigh with pleasure. Kicking off her heels, she padded over and ran her hand over the cream coverlet. At the foot of the bed, a cream-and-burgundy-striped scroll-lipped chaise followed the colour scheme of the room. A theme that was repeated in the adjoining dressing room and bathroom, right down to the burgundy-coloured tubs and bottles holding some of the most exclusive beauty products on the market.

A quick look in the dressing room confirmed the presence of her clothes. Deciding to take a shower before making the phone call, she slid out of her dress and returned to the bathroom. The urge to linger, foolishly hoping that the comforting water would wash away her troubles, was entertained for a single minute before she turned off the shower.

This wasn't the path she would have chosen for herself. For as long as she could remember, she'd relied on herself. Even her mother had warned her never to rely fully on her. The one time she'd pushed aside that warning, and thought to seek out emotional support elsewhere, namely through her absentee father, the situation had backfired spectacularly. What Ramon was demanding of her pushed all of her control-freak buttons. But she truly had no choice. Not with so much on the line.

Towelling herself dry, her hand lingered over her stomach, the constant ache in her heart still very much present, but it held one less layer of the dark despair that had triggered tears a handful of days ago. She didn't want to give in to hope. Mother Nature had dealt her the worst blow she could suffer, so hope was still a scarce commodity to her. But if nothing else, she was glad her ache was less tormenting.

Returning to the dressing room, she retrieved the nightshirt, tucked it over her head and stopped to survey the meagre contents of her wardrobe. Yet another thing she needed to deal with. Besides the light blue sundress and sweater she'd worn to travel, she'd only packed a further two dresses, her nightshirt, a handful of underwear and sandals for her three-day stay. Even she couldn't make that last for nine months.

The hysterical bubble nestling just beneath the surface of her emotions threatened to expand again.

Squashing it back down, she climbed into her sumptuous bed, picked up the bedside phone and punched the familiar number.

It was answered on the third ring. Taking a deep breath, Suki said, 'Mum, I have something to tell you.'

CHAPTER SEVEN

As POTENTIALLY LIFE-CHANGING phone calls went, her mother took the news that there could be hope health-wise for her with quiet but flat acceptance, although Suki suspected the secret fondness her mother held for Luis played a part in her accepting his offer.

Suki had deliberately left her return date vague, not wanting to overly distress her mother.

'Did you speak to your mother?'

Ramon's voice and question dragged her back to the present, to the immense dining room and the highly polished teak banquet table and high-backed chairs that could easily seat an entire state cabinet. Here too, soaring ceilings held magnificent arches and stained glass.

Before her an exquisite setting of multiple plates, glasses and silverware had been laid out for their meal, making her once again feel out of her depth.

Unbidden, Luis's face rose up before her. He would've had a laughing fit at her expense by now. Struggling to contain her sadness, she nodded at Ramon.

He'd changed out of his suit into more casual clothes, his slicked-back hair still damp from a recent shower. Although his attire was still funeral black, the long-sleeved T-shirt, pulled up to exhibit brawny arms, gave him a slightly more approachable air. Although that air was put in serious jeopardy each time she looked into his stormy eyes.

'Yes. I couldn't really tell her too much because I don't know all the details.'

'I spoke with the specialists this afternoon. They will be in touch with her doctors tomorrow and arrange to fly her to Miami in the next three days.'

Surprise spiked through her. 'That soon?'

'I'm sure you'll agree that the sooner things get moving, the better?'

He wasn't just referring to her mother.

'Yes.'

'Good. Then you'll be pleased to know I've made an appointment for us to visit a doctor in Havana tomorrow,' he said calmly as he draped his napkin over his lap. 'After that we'll fly to Miami for the day.'

Suki paused in the act of picking up her spoon to taste the heavenly smelling beef and garbanzo bean soup Teresa had served them. 'Why? My mother wouldn't have arrived by then.'

'Since we won't be busy making a baby first thing in the morning, I scheduled a meeting for the morning, while you take the necessary time to replenish your wardrobe. Unless you intend to recycle the clothes in that weekender you brought for the next year?'

The fact that she'd pondered the same problem didn't stop her lips from pursing. 'I was going to sort something small here in Havana and organise some clothes when I returned to England.'

He put the fork in his hand down carefully, his jaw set. 'You won't be returning to England until you're pregnant and since the child is to be born here, it makes sense for you to remain here. Besides, your mother will be in Miami—you can visit her any time you want.'

Suki wasn't sure whether it was his complete certainty in his own virility or the high-handed way he'd taken over her life that stuck in her craw. 'Do you intend to dictate every single second of my life from now on? Because if that's the case you and I will have a big problem.'

'Accept that I will be taking a huge part in making sure this pregnancy goes smoothly and we won't have one.'

Her fingers tightened around the spoon. 'I'm not even pregnant yet!'

'You could be by now if you weren't so touchy about having sex in broad daylight.'

She cursed her flaming face almost as much as she silently cursed him. 'Oh, my God, you really think you're a stud, don't you?'

His shrug was pure male arrogance. 'I got you pregnant the first time despite using contraceptives. I choose to believe we'll be equally lucky in conception this time round.'

'And if I don't get pregnant immediately?' she challenged.

His teeth bared in a smug smile. 'That's the great thing about sex. As long as we have the necessary functioning equipment, we can keep trying. Again and again. Now eat your soup before it goes cold.'

'I think I've lost my appetite,' she returned.

'Eat it anyway. You need to regain your full health.'

Suki wasn't sure whether to be thankful that he hadn't added *for the baby's sake* to his statement. She wasn't even sure whether it was wise to borrow a little of his dogged assurance. And although her doctors had assured her that her baby's condition wasn't in any way genetic, she couldn't dissipate the fear that continued to live in her heart.

With her mind churning anew, she didn't notice she'd finished her soup until she looked up and saw Teresa's beaming smile of approval.

Her gaze went from her empty bowl to Ramon's cocked eyebrow. 'Let's hope you've *lost your appetite* for the main course too,' he mocked.

Her eyes rolled before she could stop herself. His deep chuckle twanged, then lightened something in her midriff. Unwilling to examine what that *something* was, she sipped her water, nibbled on a piece of thick bread and searched for neutral conversation that didn't involve sex or babies.

'I thought you couldn't fly into the States from Cuba?'

'Until recently, no, you couldn't. But things are beginning to change.

She caught a note in his voice, a blend of pride and anticipation.

'I noticed a bit of regeneration going on in Havana. Is this change why you're choosing to remain in Cuba?'

His expression darkened a touch but he answered her question with a nod. 'Partly, *sí*.'

She didn't need to ask what the other part was. The deep loss he felt was stamped in his expression. His way of somewhat assuaging that loss was why she was here.

Teresa walked in then with the main course of chicken stuffed with roasted peppers and coconut rice. Again they fell into silence and Suki polished off every mouthful on her plate.

They were waiting for dessert to be served when he reached into his pocket and placed an envelope in front of her. 'I'll be taking care of your mother's medical bills, so this is yours to do with as you please.'

She picked it up and slid the folded flap open. At the sight of the cheque, she caught her breath. Then, sending a thankful prayer to her best friend, she nodded. 'Okay.'

If he was curious as to what she intended to do with it, he didn't show it. The charged atmosphere that lurked beneath the surface of their dealings kept conversation to a stiff minimum. Her questions about the doctor in Havana were answered.

The thought that she was of no further interest to Ramon save for her reproductive purpose attempted to cause a level of hurt she wasn't comfortable with, so she ruthlessly pushed it to one side.

'I know we didn't discuss this fully, but I would prefer not to give up working altogether. Sitting around all day will drive me insane.'

She fully expected another disagreement, but to her surprise he pushed back his chair and rose.

'I have a project you could work on, once everything else is taken care of.'

Her eyes widened, a tiny spurt of pleasure welling inside her. 'You do?'

He nodded. 'Come.'

Dropping her napkin on the table, she followed him out of the dining room. Her nap and his late arrival had put a spanner in the tour he'd promised earlier but she'd conducted a mini tour of her own when one of the staff members had led her down for dinner. Each room she'd glanced into had been more spectacular than the last. So she was sure Ramon's project didn't involve the villa.

Until she walked into the room in the west wing. The difference was so jarring, so very *wrong* that her jaw dropped.

'My God, who did this?'

'Someone I had no business trusting,' he replied.

The room, another salon but this one opening onto a terrace facing the sparkling pool and designed to catch the best of the evening sun, had been turned into a futuristic minimalist nightmare completely at odds with the rest of the villa. Everywhere she looked blinding white furniture clashed with chrome and chintz.

'Why did you give them the project, then?' she asked, unsure whether to shut her eyes against the garish design or cry for the indignity the room had suffered.

When he didn't answer immediately, she looked away from the aluminium hanging fireplace to where he leaned against the lintel.

'I went against my better judgement. I also, erroneously, gave them carte blanche. When I realised my mistake I called a halt to it. As you can see, everything came to an untimely standstill.'

She glanced at the far wall, noticing that it was only half done. 'How did they take you firing them mid-project?'

His mouth twitched but it was with something other than humour. 'I got them to see that our differences of opinion were deeply ingrained in fundamental issues and that it was best we parted ways immediately.'

She walked further into the room, mourning the plain walls where beautiful stained glass and intricate carvings should've been. 'I can't believe they did...this! Did you manage to save any of the original features?'

To her surprise, he nodded. 'Teresa's husband, Mario, is the caretaker. He had the wherewithal to ensure everything taken from here was kept intact. Are you interested in a restoration project?'

She gasped. 'Of course! My last big job was a restoration on a country house in Sussex. It wasn't as big as this or anywhere near as intricate but I'd love to sink my teeth into this, if you're okay with that?'

'I'm okay with that. Mario will show you where he stored the stone and other features. But this will happen only—'

'When I've fulfilled my other duties. I know.'

His lids descended over his eyes for a minute before he walked further into the room. Stopping before her, he said, 'The tour I promised will have to wait. I have a few more calls to make and we have an early start tomorrow. I want you rested.'

Despite the heat crawling up her neck, she returned his gaze. 'You don't need to keep doing that, Ramon.'

One eyebrow lifted. 'Keep doing what?'

'Reminding me that we'll be…that I'll be…'

'Taking my seed into your body come tomorrow night?' he finished helpfully, not an ounce of embarrassment in sight.

She reddened fiercer. 'Oh, my God, who talks like that?'

He ignored the question, his fingers rising to

trace her hot cheek. 'You blush so readily, *guapa.* One could be fooled into thinking you're one step removed from the very angels.' The observation was flat, but tinged with a definite thread of censure.

And just like that the lighter mood was gone.

'If anyone chooses to make assumptions about me, that's their problem. I never claimed to be angelic. But I'm also not the heartless devil you think I am. I'm sorry that you see me that way.'

His fingers snaked past her jaw and beneath her loose hair to cup her nape. 'Are you?'

Having seen the pain he was in, a part of her understood his emotions. 'Yes, I am.'

'That remains to be seen, I guess.'

Her heart quaked. Resolutely, she stepped away. 'Don't forget those calls you need to go and make.'

He stayed where he was, watching her for a further minute. *'Buenas noches,* Suki.'

She didn't respond. The emotions surging into her throat wouldn't let her. So she stood silently as he walked out of the room. Then, unable to stay in the starkly minimalist apology for a room, she walked out of the French doors onto the pillared terrace.

Down a short flight of stairs the under-lit swimming pool glinted invitingly. The night air cooled her on the outside but, inside, she was still reeling from Ramon's words. By the events of the day.

Ramon had never answered her question about how long he'd known about the baby, but if he'd discussed it with Luis then he'd known for a few months. She shuddered to think how long he'd held on to his anger. How long he intended to hold her in such an unforgiving light. Until she gave him another child?

How could they even make love when there was such acrimony between them?

I don't need to like you to take you to bed. And vice versa.

Recalling the words sent another shiver through her, along with the disarming acceptance that it was true. Although he'd apologised for his uncouth comments, he hadn't exactly been bursting with poetry and roses that night ten months ago.

And she, regardless of his lack of warmth, hadn't minded in the least. Her body had thrilled to his touch, had lapped up every particle of attention he'd generously delivered to her.

Her escalating heartbeat now mocked her with that remembered thrill. Mocked her with the fact that he only had to touch her for her senses to threaten to dive into free fall. The cold, hard truth was that making love with Ramon even for the clinical sake of conceiving a child wouldn't be the most difficult thing she would ever do.

But the risk to her soul, the knowledge that this could all emotionally backfire spectacularly if she wasn't careful, stayed with her long after she'd returned to her suite and slid beneath the sheets.

She was up and showered and in the dining room by eight the next morning, one of the maids having gently woken her a little after seven with the instruction that the *señor* wished to leave by nine. She chose to see it as a blessing that Ramon hadn't hammered on her door himself with that command.

She had almost finished her breakfast when he walked in. Today, his attire was a little less severe, the dark grey suit and lighter grey shirt bringing out the vibrancy of his skin and eyes. Those eyes, however, were no less sombre when they raked over her simple off-white, off-the-shoulder sundress and the neat ponytail she'd tied her hair in.

'*Buenos días, cara.* You look as well rested as I feel,' he observed dryly.

Since she'd spent most of the night tossing and turning, she knew his statement was less than flattering. Her chest tightened. 'I see you're brimming with compliments this morning.'

'Perhaps I'm feeling less than generous because

our night could've been put to better use than counting sheep.'

She shrugged, experiencing a tiny burst of pride when it came off smoothly. 'I didn't count sheep. The spectacular wall carvings in my room were a much better visual distraction.'

He paused in the act of pouring steaming black coffee, a flash of something dark and carnal passing through his eyes. 'I hope you enjoyed them because you won't be inspecting them tonight,' he promised, the raw intent in his eyes making her belly quiver.

Suki refrained from voicing another objection to the blatant reminder. Hadn't she woken up this morning thinking exactly the same thing? And hadn't that knowledge sent darts of secret anticipation straight between her thighs?

Carefully, she set down her half-finished cup of tea and stood. 'I'm done. I'll go and grab my bag and I'll be ready to go.'

Without looking at her, he picked up the folded newspaper next to his plate and snapped it open. 'Changing the subject won't make the event disappear, *cara*.'

'No, but discussing it ad nauseam will definitely make it tedious.'

He perused the inside of the first page. 'Are you calling me boring, Suki?' he murmured.

'I'm calling you out on the fact that, for someone who is lauded for his intelligence, you seem to have developed a one-track mind.'

That got his attention. He looked up from the paper, ferocious green eyes lancing her. 'I get that way when there's something I'm passionate about,' he replied in a low, ardently dangerous voice. 'And on this subject, rest assured that I am *extremely* passionate.'

He returned to his paper, the silently dismissive gesture freeing her to leave the room. She did so swiftly, perhaps even admitting she was fleeing from contemplating what it would feel like to have Ramon be passionate about something other than sex. Be passionate about *her*.

No. Her stupid crush had died long before she'd been beset with the heartbreaking news of her unborn child's illness. It had taken a giant knock when she'd woken up alone the morning after their night together. It'd died the day she'd discovered he'd lied to her about Svetlana.

That welcome reminder threw cold water on her rioting emotions, thankfully, as she freshened up and collected her bag.

He was on the phone when she returned. He got

off long enough to attend the lawyers who'd once again been summoned, this time to witness her agreement with Ramon. For a startling second she wondered which other agreements Ramon had got them to draw up that they didn't seem in any way surprised by hers, but then she pushed the useless thought away. Her situation was hers alone to deal with.

Ramon stopped long enough to lock the agreement in the safe in his study. Then, with the next few years of her life committed to the man who looked at her with a fair amount of dislike, she followed him out onto the helipad.

For most of the helicopter flight back to Havana, he made one call after another. For the sake of discretion, Ramon informed her, the trio of doctors were summoned to the Acosta suite at Ramon's hotel. For a solid hour, she answered questions about her health, had her blood drawn and her pressure recorded.

She believed they were done when the doctor powered down his tablet, only to see Ramon taking his place in the chair she'd just vacated. Surprised, she watched him roll his sleeves up in preparation for his own vitals to be taken.

He caught her look and returned it with a steady

one of his own. 'My last health check was satisfactory. But it doesn't hurt to be doubly sure, does it?'

Numbly, she shook her head. When he turned away to answer the doctor's questions in low-toned Spanish, she retreated to the far side of the living room. Staring down at the bustling street below, Suki refused to entertain the strange sensation zipping through her stomach.

Not only was Ramon deadly serious about having this child, he was going the extra mile to ensure he was in optimum health. Why that should make her insides sing, she didn't want to examine too closely. Or at all. So she wouldn't.

Unfortunately, her senses weren't in a listening mood. She was veering down the path of wondering what sort of father Ramon would make when she sensed him coming up behind her.

She turned to find him lowering his sleeve over a thick, tanned, hair-sprinkled arm. And for the life of her she couldn't stop staring at it. At him. Like that night in the limo, her senses were swerving into dangerous territory, her nostrils flaring wider to breathe more of his intoxicating scent as he stopped in front of her.

'We're done here. Are you ready to go?'

'Yes,' she said, cringing at the huskiness of her voice.

Get yourself together!

She stepped to one side and smiled her thanks at the doctors before they took their leave. Then she headed for the door herself. Lingering in this suite with Ramon wasn't safe. Not when every move he made drew its own brand of fascination from her. Not when there was a more than adequately functioning king-sized bed so close by.

If he sensed her fresh agitation, he didn't give an indication of it. By the time he joined her at the lift, his impeccable clothes were in place.

'The tests will be expedited. We should have the preliminary ones by this evening although I'm not expecting any surprises.'

Or anything to stand in his way.

She chose not to touch the unvoiced words.

They emerged into sunlight and the awaiting limo. Half an hour later, they were at the airport. This time she didn't need prompting to get out of the car. The tension of yesterday underlined newer, even riskier tension. The kind that made her stomach flutter wildly each time Ramon so much as glanced her way.

Something he seemed to do often, despite the long phone call he was engaged in for most of the journey.

As for that beautifully lilted Spanish that fell so smoothly from his lips?

Dear heaven, she was losing it.

It didn't help that she was robbed of further breath the moment she stepped into his private jet. Every corner of the plane was decked out with unapologetic comfort and luxury in mind. Silky leather suede in soft accents covered all three separate groupings of sofas and armchairs. Light-coloured marble lined the table tops and flat-screen TVs broadcasted the latest financial and world news from two different screens. The two attendants and pilots who greeted them wore the same Acosta Hotels logo on their uniforms that she'd seen previously, and the English they greeted her with was impeccable.

Feeling more than a little out of place in her simple dress and sandals, Suki slowed as she reached the middle of the plane. The touch of a firm, warm hand at her waist made her jump, her senses screeching as Ramon turned her to face him.

'You need to take a seat so we can take off.'

Nodding stiffly, she started to move towards an armchair. The hand at her waist checked her progress and steered her towards a two-seater sofa. Pressing her into it, he buckled her in and sat down next to her, bringing one lean, powerful thigh much too close to her own. Under the pretext of crossing her legs, she shifted away.

A quick glance at him showed he'd caught the movement. And wasn't terribly impressed with it.

'Ramon…' She wasn't exactly sure what she'd hoped to say but one attendant approached them with drinks. She accepted a fruit punch, took a sip of the refreshing drink while Ramon chose a mineral water.

He waited until they were alone again to slice her with a dark look. 'It would be good if you didn't jump like a startled rabbit when I touch you in public.'

'I wasn't aware that we would be doing public outings together,' she replied.

His mouth twisted. 'Did you think I was going to hide you away for the next nine months?'

She hadn't thought of that. To be honest, the swiftly ticking clock, racing towards what would happen tonight, hadn't given her much thinking room since she woke up this morning. 'But aren't you worried that it'll send out a certain impression?' she asked, a little bubble of bemusement taking root inside.

'What sort of impression?'

She licked nervous lips. 'Well…people are going to think we're together.'

He shrugged, eyeing her with a steady look. 'I don't have a problem with that. Do you?'

No. *Yes.* She shook her head in confusion. 'But we're not. I don't like people assuming something that isn't true.'

'What would you suggest? That we take out an ad in the paper stating that we're having sex simply to have a child together?'

She glared at him. 'No, of course not.'

'You and I know the truth. That's all that matters.' The words held a ring of intractable finality.

Suki was reeling long after their plane had launched itself into the sky. For better or worse, her life was tied to Ramon's for the foreseeable future.

CHAPTER EIGHT

HE WASN'T GOING to demand to know what was going on in her head. Nor was he going to demand conversation. And the need to reach out and free her thick caramel-blonde hair from the ponytail was certainly one he wouldn't be indulging.

He had achieved his purpose where Suki was concerned. Or as near enough to it without having performed the act itself.

She'd subsided into near silence after their conversation on the plane, only acknowledging him when he deposited her in his private suite at Acosta Hotel Miami and left for his meeting. By then he'd concluded that talking was no longer necessary, or even a pleasurable experience with her. Half the time she argued with him. The other half she offered sympathy or touched on subjects that he found difficult. All the time his attention was absorbed by her animation, the little gestures with her hand she probably wasn't aware she was making.

All distracting and frankly irritating.

So for now, he would enjoy the peace of mind afforded to him as he sat in the VIP dressing area of the top Miami stylist his assistant had scheduled Suki to visit.

A visit he'd accompanied her on simply because his mid-afternoon meeting had wrapped up early. Grabbing a copy of the financial paper he hadn't been able to finish at breakfast this morning, he tuned out the three attendants' hushed debate about which signature style to create for Suki.

The woman in question was seated on a chaise longue at the opposite end of the room, her shapely legs neatly crossed at the ankles. She was choosing not to participate in the conversation. Even looked borderline bored, a shrug very much in her expression each time she was asked a question.

Ramon's irritation grew. Every woman he'd dated previously, without exception, had been an utter slave to shopping, the more exclusive, the more fervent the rhapsody. And the more adoring gratitude had come his way.

Suki looked as if she would have more fun watching paint dry.

Her gaze met his. Her lips pursed and her eyes stayed wide and unblinking. The distinct notion that she was fighting the urge to roll her eyes startled, then amused him.

Fighting the sudden twitch of his own lips, he returned his attention to his paper.

Eventually, the whole ensemble headed for an inner sanctum.

For five minutes he read and re-read the same article on the price of soya. The door opened. He tossed the paper aside.

The dress was a bold blood-red, the material a floor-length affair that clung to her body from chest to knees, leaving her shoulders bare and outlining her hourglass figure to perfection. Absently he heard one stylist refer to it as a Bardot-style evening dress.

With her hair caught back, her elegant neck and delicate shoulders gave off a fragile look he knew was false. Suki Langston had a backbone of steel. And as much as the reason for her presence in his life disturbed him, he couldn't deny the fact that her beauty was enthralling. That the hot tug in his groin that had perturbed and then shamelessly dogged him with each subsequent time they'd met wasn't going to go away.

He caught her full reflection in the mirror as one attendant stepped out of the way. She was smoothing her hand down her midriff. When it paused at her stomach, the place where his child had briefly been cradled, something hard and agonising pierced his chest.

The need to see his seed grow there, watch her belly expand with his child, filled every cell in his body.

The hell he'd lived in since finding out about his child, and the further agony of losing the family he'd never thought would be taken from him so suddenly, reared up and knocked him sideways.

He didn't realise he'd made a sound until all four women froze and glanced his way. Suki's gaze met his in the mirror and he caught the faintest tremble in her lips and sympathy in her vivid blue eyes.

He wanted to reject it, wanted to snarl that he didn't need it. But his eyes stayed on hers, silently and secretly absorbing the sentiment.

'She'll take that one,' he rasped into the silence.

The innocuous words altered the mood. A flurry of activity ensued. Having achieved success with the first dress, the stylist decided his opinion was needed for every subsequent ensemble.

He approved another half a dozen evening dresses, growled his dislike of a metallic gold cocktail dress that clung a little too tightly and showed off a little too much skin. At some point it was decided she would take her hair down to better judge the true style of one dress. The sight of her free-flowing hair sent another burst of heat through his bloodstream.

He was nodding at her selection of swimsuits and daywear when his phone rang. The doctors' news sent a bolt of satisfaction through him. Followed closely by ramped-up anticipation.

The next call was to his American pilot to ready his plane.

Suki caught the tail end of the conversation. Enquiring blue eyes met his. He infused purpose in his gaze and watched her swallow.

Rising, he quickly brought the spree to a conclusion and led her out of the boutique with more than a little haste.

'Any reason why we're hotfooting it out of here like we're fleeing the scene of a crime?' she asked, but the hitch in her voice and the furtive glance his way suggested she already guessed the answer.

'Our preliminary tests have returned with a green light,' he answered as they settled into the car.

'So...?'

'So we're returning home, Suki. I've waited long enough.' Once he'd dragged himself from the depths of grief and accepted that only the promise of an heir would assuage him, he'd been planning for this event. He felt zero qualms about the swiftness with which he was moving now success was in his sights. The yearning stamped in his blood needed to be answered. Right now.

He couldn't bring his brother or parents back, but he could ensure their memories lived on through his child.

The journey back was swift and uneventful. Not so much the palpable tension that rose between them the moment they stepped off the plane and onto his helicopter.

Ramon told himself that the anticipation firing through his veins was born of the primal need to ensure his family and legacy survived the tragic circumstances that had befallen him.

But as the rotors beat relentlessly towards his villa, he realised the woman too counted. For whatever reason nature saw fit, the chemistry between Suki and him transcended all logical explanation. Svetlana might have committed the physical act of cheating on him with other men, but in the handful of times he'd interacted with Suki when Luis had attended a function with her, the evidence of the unmistakable chemistry between them had caused Ramon more than a hint of discomfort.

Perhaps that had been the reason he'd acted so deplorably on the night of her birthday. Entering the pub and seeing Luis holding her hand had unexpectedly jarred. Recognising the emotion as dark rancid jealousy hadn't improved a mood that had already been in a black pit after discovering the true extent of Svetlana's infidelity. Perhaps taking Suki to bed that night had been his own way of salving the indignity to his manhood and pride.

For sure, he'd woken up in the early hours more than a little unimpressed with his behaviour. Not enough that he'd regretted the hours he'd spent in Suki's bed. But enough to know that retreat was best for everyone in that moment.

He glanced at her now, completely certain there would be no retreat now.

She was his.

At least until she bore him a child. What came after that would be decided when the time was right.

He took her hand the moment the helicopter landed in Cienfuegos. He noted the slight lag in her steps and suppressed the apprehension that rose within him. She'd barely touched her food on the plane and her eyes had grown steadily darker and her face pinched.

Dios. Anyone would think she was a virgin headed for the slaughter. Wasn't she though, to all intents and purposes? She'd only had one previous lover bar him. One sexual encounter. The primitive part of the alpha male in him had been more than thrilled at that admission, but he hadn't failed to notice her lack of experience on their first night together.

His racing libido throttled down a notch. Entering the main salon, he pulled her to a stop before him. Despite her heeled sandals, she needed to tilt her head to meet his gaze.

So small.

Yet so strong.

His gaze drifted over her, fresh hunger clawing through him, but he couldn't ignore the obvious.

'You're nervous,' he observed.

She laughed self-deprecatingly. 'Give the man a prize.'

'Have you forgotten that we've done this before?'

If anything, her tension increased. 'After which you left my bedroom without so much as an *adios*, if I recall.' Her voice was hushed, but there was a strained note in it that was more than the hurt he sensed.

Ramon got the distinct impression he'd been judged and found wanting, which shouldn't have surprised him considering his own admission of his less than stellar conduct. But still, a thousand tiny pinpricks dragged over his skin. 'A lot of what happened that night was…unfortunate.'

Her face tightened. Her eyelashes dropped to fan her cheeks. 'I see.'

He caught and lifted her chin with his finger. 'But not what happened in the car, or in your bed,' he clarified firmly.

Her face remained closed. 'I don't really see the point in dissecting it any more. What happened… happened.'

Ramon should've been pleased. He wasn't.

Letting go of her, he walked to the drinks cabinet. About to pour them both a drink, he hesitated. Alcohol was a hard *no* for her considering what they were trying to achieve. And he would do well to keep his wits about him.

About to suggest an alternative, he stopped when she glanced at the door. 'I'm going upstairs to… um…take a shower.'

Great idea, he wanted to say, but one look at her face told him she intended it to be a solo mission.

Suppressing the torrid images, for now, he nodded. 'I'll be up shortly.'

She opened her mouth, as if to contradict him, but, face still set in unhappy lines, she walked out of the room.

He shoved a hand through his hair.

Dios. Maybe he would have that drink after all.

The shot of cognac did nothing to bring clarity or calm his raging need.

He'd spent the months after Svetlana's betrayal burying himself in work and avoiding any and all liaisons. Not because he'd been heartbroken, but because he'd realised how jaded the idea of relationships had grown for him.

He and Luis had been lucky enough to grow up in a stable and happy home. Although not wealthy, their parents had ensured they got the best education, his half-American mother smoothing the way for them to attend top universities in the States.

It was this solid foundation he'd foolishly thought to emulate with Svetlana, despite the clear evidence that successful marriages, especially among wealthy men like him, were rare. How many of his silver-spoon college buddies had come from broken homes and were themselves intent on living duplicitous lives even before they'd entered the real world?

After Svetlana, he'd even been a little disconcerted to realise sex had grown boring for him and the idea of pursuing a woman had dropped to an all-time low on his list.

All that apathy was nowhere in sight right now.

He paced the salon, nursing a second drink while keeping an eye on the clock.

Ten minutes later, he set the crystal tumbler down and strode from the room. The knock on her door produced no response. That unsettling irritation that was never far off dogged him again. Turning the handle, he tried the door, exhaling when it yielded to his push.

He was getting somewhere if she hadn't locked him out. Except she wasn't in the bedroom and there was no sound from the bathroom.

The absurd idea that she'd made a run for it had him charging for the French doors that led to her private terrace. His hand was on the doorknob when he heard a faint sound behind him.

'Ramon?'

He turned.

She was framed in the doorway of her dressing room, clad in only a towel. Her face glowed a light pink from her shower and her damp hair tumbled around her naked shoulders. With no make-up, no sexy lingerie or perfumed skin to entice, Ramon wondered how she could still be the most captivating woman he'd ever encountered.

Because, *Madre de Dios*, she was.

Blood and lust thrumming wildly through his veins, he slowly moved towards her, watched her fingers twist in a death grip on the knot of the towel.

Her gaze flitted from his to the French doors before rushing back to his, as if, like him, she couldn't look away for long enough. 'Did you just break into my bedroom?'

He gave a low laugh. 'I was checking to make sure you hadn't decided to make a run for it.'

He stopped before her, breathing in the intoxicating scent of woman.

His woman.

'And if I had?'

'I would've chased you down,' he vowed.

A shiver trembled through her. He wanted to trace his fingers over her satin-smooth skin, elicit another delicious shiver. But if he touched her that way, here in this room, he wouldn't be able to stop.

Closing the gap between them, he caught her around the waist. Lifting her high, he banded one arm around her and started to walk.

One hand landed on his shoulder to steady herself as her eyes widened. 'Where...where are we going?'

He passed through the open door and took a right towards the end of the corridor. 'I've had you in my car and in your bed. This time I'm taking you in *my* bed.'

Her breath hitched in a sexy little rush that went straight to his groin. Striding through his private living room into his bedroom, he kicked the door shut with his foot and set her down.

'Let go of the towel,' he rasped in a voice he barely recognised as his own.

She blinked, then looked around wildly before her gaze returned to his. Whatever she saw in his face made her draw her lower lip between her teeth and worry it mercilessly.

Ramon barely managed to stop the torturous groan that rumbled up from his chest.

'Drop the towel, Suki. Or I'll do it for you,' he growled.

Despite the alarming widening of her eyes, she shook her head. 'You take something off first.'

He sighed. 'Are we going to argue about every single thing?'

The hand gripping the towel tightened defiantly. 'Equality is a very big thing for women these days.'

His mouth attempted to lift without his permission but the severity of his need killed his mirth. His jacket came off and hit the floor, followed by his tie and shirt.

When his hand went to his belt, she froze, her gaze following the movement. He slowed the slide of the belt through the loops. Something about having her eyes on him turned him on even harder.

He hadn't forgotten his paramount objective but, *Dios*, he was also going to take a little bit of pleasure in his task.

'*Do it*, Suki. I won't tell you again.'

Slowly, she let go of the towel.

Everything locked inside him, save for the electric zap of lust that powered his every cell. Maybe he was going to take more than a little pleasure in bringing his child into the world.

Discarding the belt, he pulled her into his arms, fisted one hand in her thick hair, angled her face up to his. The wave of anxiety that crossed her face pulled him short for a moment.

'This can be the clinical exercise you accused it of being. Or we can attempt to enjoy it. Which would you prefer?'

Her mouth fell open in shock, then she blushed fiercely. 'I...how can I answer that without...without...?'

He glided his thumb over her lips. 'It's fine, you don't need to incriminate yourself. *I* would prefer the latter. And I will proceed accordingly unless you indicate otherwise.'

'Or we can stop dissecting it and just get on with

it?' she muttered, her colour heightening as her gaze dropped from his.

Ramon wanted to bring it back to his. But he couldn't resist the prompt to *just get on with it*. Not when his hands were gliding over her glorious skin and her breathing was altering in that heady way again. Not when the sight of the tip of her tongue caressing her inner lip was threatening to drive him insane.

The distance to his bed was mercifully short. Laying her down, he quickly disposed of his remaining clothes. When her wide-eyed gaze took in his erection, he swallowed a groan and brought himself under fierce control.

Stretching out next to her, he pressed her body to his, caressed his hand down the delicate line of her spine.

She arched against him, bringing the tips of her sweet breasts against his chest. When the sensitised tips brushed him, she whimpered. The sound, like every single one she made, drove blood straight between his legs.

Unable to resist, he bent his head and took one pink peak into his mouth. Her whimper turned into a cry as her fingers spiked through his hair.

Sí, there was absolutely no reason why they

couldn't enjoy making this baby that would ensure the continuation of his family's legacy.

In pathetically few minutes, the insane hunger threatened to annihilate him.

Pressing her onto her back, he braced himself over her.

Suki didn't think she had any more air in her lungs to exhale with as Ramon parted her thighs. But apparently the sight of him, crouched so masterfully over her, could elicit another giddy rush of air.

She couldn't...*shouldn't* be enjoying this. Every particle in her body shouldn't be craving what was coming so much. And yet wild, dizzy anticipation continued to ripple through her as his fingers slid between their bodies, located that needy place between her thighs and delivered wicked caresses.

Her head was rolling restlessly on his pillow as he started kissing his way down her body. Openmouthed kisses that branded her skin and left a trail of fire she was sure would never be extinguished. She wasn't aware her nails were digging into his shoulders until he hissed encouragement.

Dragging her head off the pillow, she looked down to find his ferocious gaze pinned on her, tracking her every response.

He got to her belly and he paused, his lips hovering over her womb. An enigmatic expression washed over his face. Then his head dropped one last fraction, anointing her belly with a kiss. Something heavy and indefinable moved through her, wrapped around her heart.

Suki shied away from it, her intuition pushing her towards emotional self-preservation. His mouth brushed lower and she stopped thinking altogether.

She resurfaced from her first climax long enough to feel him tug her resolutely beneath him.

'Open your eyes, Suki,' he rasped above her.

She dragged heavy lids open, her chest rising and falling rapidly. His eyes were a dark, primitive green. The turbulence surging through her was reflected perfectly in his gaze.

His hand barely slid beneath her to hold her steady before he thrust inside her. 'Oh!'

His harsh exhalation reverberated in the room. Burying himself to the hilt, he held himself still, fine tremors shaking through his body as his teeth clenched. The sight of him fighting for control thrilled a shamelessly feminine part of her.

Enough for her to raise her hand and slide her fingers over his rigid stubbled jaw, through his hair, drag her nails along his scalp, sink them into his nape.

A guttural groan ripped free from his throat as he began to move. Powerfully. Relentlessly. His possession was masterful and thorough, commanding every single cell in her body by the time the glorious pressure threatened to stop her breathing.

Frantic for an anchor, her hands found his waist, dug in and stayed as he hurled her relentlessly to the edge.

'Ramon...'

'*Sí, guapa.* Give in,' he encouraged throatily.

She didn't need a second bidding. Shameless cries ripped from her own throat as bliss burst wild and free from deep within her.

Seconds later, Ramon gave an animalistic growl above her before he rammed deep...deeper than he'd ever been inside her. The sensation of his seed filling her, flooding her, shook new, alien feeling inside her long after their breaths had returned to normal. Long after he'd rolled to the side and tucked her against him.

That band around her heart, the one that held apprehension and a whole lot more sensation than she could fathom right now, tightened even further. She tried to will it away. But it loomed larger until she couldn't stem the feeling morphing into naked fear in her chest.

When she pulled free, he let her go.

Her duty was done. At least for tonight. She moved to the edge of the bed, swung her legs down.

Before she could stand, a thick arm snagged her waist, dragged her back against the sheets.

'Where do you think you're going?' he demanded. His sculpted cheekbones were still flushed and his hair was in total disarray. But he remained sinfully, impossibly gorgeous, his face threatening her equilibrium all over again. She fought it with every spare ounce of control she could summon.

'I'm returning to my room.'

'No, you're not. Until we get a positive result you're sleeping in this bed every night. I will have your things moved here tomorrow.'

She was shaking her head before he'd finished. 'I… I would rather not.'

His face closed, his displeasure evident. 'If you think I'm hunting you down every night, think again.'

'Hunting me down? I'm right next door.'

'Then save us both the trouble of maintaining separate rooms.'

She shook her head again, her instincts screaming that this was a terrible idea.

He exhaled impatiently. 'If you insist on your

feminine independence, you can shower and dress in your own suite. But when I'm in this room so will you. Agreed?'

This was his idea of a compromise. She could waste her breath arguing. Or she could take the offer. She took the offer. 'Agreed.'

His expression changed into one of hard satisfaction. Leaning down, he delivered a firm, swift kiss on her lips before he raised his head a fraction. 'One more thing.'

'Yes?' she replied shakily.

'You attempting to leave my bed so soon leads me to think you believe I'll be taking you just once a night.' His lips brushed hers as he spoke, trailing little bursts of fire on her tingling mouth. 'Am I right, *cara*?' he enquired huskily.

Her face flamed. 'I wasn't… I didn't give it that much thought.'

His tight-lipped smile mocked her. 'Well, in case it crossed your mind, revise that impression, *guapa*. And also revise the notion that I will be restricting myself to only nights from now on.'

She was flailing under the torrent of his words when his hand slid down to boldly cup her hip. Before she could so much as take a breath, he had once again taken control of her body.

CHAPTER NINE

RAMON ACOSTA WAS a man on a mission. That became very clear, very quickly. If she slept for more than two or three hours at a stretch during the night, she called that a victory. And he didn't restrict himself to just the bedroom. Discovering her enjoying a mid-morning decaf coffee on his private terrace after lingering in bed for the morning, he'd calmly reefed off his T-shirt and paint-splattered sweat pants, stretched out beside her and pulled her negligee off her body. Afterwards, he'd carried her back to bed and started all over again.

The shower in her own suite had been another scene of his mastery. He'd tracked her there under some now forgotten pretext, invited himself into the steamy cubicle and proceeded to make her shower an unforgettable one.

That had been a week ago. A week when, in between bouts of intense lovemaking, he either spent equally intense hours ruling his kingdom from his study or disappearing into his studio on the boundary of his villa.

He'd given Suki the grand tour of all twenty-eight rooms of his villa the morning after they returned from Miami. Room after room had produced gasps of awe, as priceless antiques vied for attention beneath even more exquisitely carved stone and wood and beautifully cut glass, but, although he'd told her what the glass-roofed structure was, he hadn't invited her inside his studio. What he had revealed was that his parents had also lived in this villa with him. The west wing where they'd had their rooms was slowly being cleared by Teresa and Mario, and Suki had chosen to stay out of their way.

It was also during that tour that she'd discovered there were two further rooms—a smaller dining room and a drawing room—that needed to be restored. Although her heart mourned the atrocity done to the rooms, she welcomed the opportunity to dwell on something else other than whether she was even now carrying Ramon's child.

But by mutual tacit agreement, neither of them had brought up the subject of pregnancy tests. Suki shied away from the wicked voice that suggested that she didn't want to know just yet so she didn't have to give up her presence in Ramon's bed. They would know soon enough when her cycle rolled around next week.

Until then, she busied herself by compiling a list of Cuban architects and restorers, conducting videoconference interviews to see who would be a good fit. And when her mother arrived in Miami, she made the trip, spending all day with Moira and Mrs Baron. Suki had been shocked to find her retired neighbour at her mother's bedside in Miami, but the older woman had been full of praise for a 'considerate' Ramon, who hadn't thought twice about making arrangements for her to accompany her friend. Suki's expressed gratitude when she'd met Ramon at the hotel afterwards had been shrugged off and quickly dismissed before he'd whisked her into the bedroom.

Her own mother had, predictably, reserved judgement, more concerned with why Suki was still in Cuba. The half-lie that she was working on a commission for Ramon hadn't sat well with her. But the bald truth would've distressed her mother even more.

So instead she'd discussed antique wallpapers and colour swatches and rhapsodised about the beauty of Luis's childhood home.

The call to her boss to request an extended leave of absence had gone more smoothly than she'd hoped. Whether or not it was aided by the tabloid pictures of her and Ramon, first at the memorial and then coming out of the boutique in Miami that had the paparazzi speculating about their relationship, she didn't know.

Charlotte Chapman, the tough but fair boss who'd hired her straight after her internship, had all but offered to keep her job open for as long as Suki needed. Unsure what the future held for her, she'd expressed her gratitude to Charlotte and promised that, yes, she would update her on a regular basis.

She was still bemused by the call when Ramon found her in the living room shortly after. A raised-brow query had prompted a retelling of the phone call. He'd given a very Latin shrug and deftly changed the subject.

That had been the first inkling that there were some subjects Ramon would pursue to the ends of the earth and others he wouldn't waste a single breath on. One such subject was the amount of clothes that had arrived two days after their visit to Miami. Even the clothes he'd initially disapproved of were included in the dozens of boxes that arrived by helicopter.

And tonight, he'd specifically picked the metallic gold dress he'd all but sneered at in the boutique.

They were supposed to be dining by candlelight on his private terrace, yet half an hour after Teresa had set out their meal he hadn't turned up.

Walking to the edge of the terrace, she glanced over to his studio. Lights blazed through the glass. She debated for a second, then went back into the bedroom. Throwing a light shawl over her dress, she left the suite.

Her flats were almost noiseless on the stone path as she approached the studio doors. The hand she raised to knock froze at the steady stream of Spanish curses that ripped through the air, followed by the sound of wood breaking. Then another.

Biting her lip, she remained caught between the urge to find out if Ramon was all right and the urge to flee.

That was how he found her minutes later when he almost ripped the door off his hinges in restless fury.

Green eyes latched on to her. '*Por el amor de—* what are you doing here?' he growled, low and dangerous.

She glanced behind him, caught a glimpse of the carnage on the studio floor. 'I…we were supposed to have dinner forty minutes ago. I came to see if you…are you okay?'

He continued to stare at her as if she were an

alien. Stepping out, he pulled the door shut behind him. 'I'm fine. My apologies for keeping you waiting,' he said stiffly, clawing a hand through his hair. 'Give me five minutes and I'll be with you.'

Questions tripped on the tip of her tongue, but the dismissal was clear. She returned to the villa, and, true to his word, he joined her five minutes later.

She turned from the terrace wall, and for a moment she thought he'd been struck dumb when he saw her.

The risqué cut of the dress negated the use of a bra, but, of course, what had looked a little daring but ultimately controllable in front of her mirror soon became a clingy, body-exposing and heat-inducing scrap of torture the moment Ramon laid his sizzling eyes on her.

Calmly he strode forward, pulled out her chair and saw her seated. But despite his attempt at easy conversation, tension poured off him. Whether it was from what she'd witnessed outside his studio or what she was wearing, she didn't dare ask, seeing as she was fighting her ultra-sensitive body's reaction to his every look.

When she attempted to surreptitiously hide the fact that her nipples had peaked to blatant points beneath the sheer silk, he set his wine glass down and decisively drew away the arm she was attempting to use to hide her body's reaction.

'We're alone, Suki. Stop hiding yourself from me.'

Her lips twisted in a tight grimace. 'This dress was a bad idea.'

'Only as a test of fortitude and patience, *belleza*. But we will persevere,' he replied drolly, although she noted the tightness of his jaw and the way he shifted in his seat every few minutes when his gaze dropped to her chest.

He waited until she'd returned to using both hands to tuck into her spicy chicken and sautéed potatoes served with a mango and avocado sauce before he returned his attention to his own food. Pleading with her body to calm down, she attempted to be content with the fact that wherever her appetite had gone it was coming back with gusto.

Ramon, on the other hand, ate less and drank more, his jaw clenching and unclenching until she resolutely set down her cutlery.

'Either my dress is bothering you more than you want to admit or something's wrong. Maybe something that involves you smashing up your studio?' she enquired boldly.

He tensed further. When he didn't reply immediately, she thought he meant to ignore her. But then he shrugged. 'I'm an artist. I'm allowed a temperamental outburst every now and then.'

'I suppose, except you look like you want to have another one right now. So I'm guessing it wasn't cathartic?'

His eyes narrowed on her, but he answered, 'I get that way when my vision and my process don't converge as they should.'

'Artist's block?'

He grimaced, his gaze sweeping her body before he glanced away. 'I prefer...frustrated.'

'How long has it been?' she asked, then mentally kicked herself. With all he'd suffered, was it a surprise?

'I drew my last painting eight months ago. My last sculpture has been even longer.'

Before his devastating loss. *But after his breakup with Svetlana?*

The food in her mouth congealed. Had the breakup affected him to the extent his art had suffered? As she watched him gulp back another mouthful of red wine, his features set, Suki's chest tightened.

Silence reigned while he took another sip.

'Since we're sharing intimate subjects, which of your parents decided to name you Suki?' he asked.

She looked up, a little startled at the unexpected

question. Then, glad for the change of subject, she smiled. 'My mother. It was her favourite teacher's name. She decided from a young age that she would name her daughter that.'

'And your father didn't raise any objection?' he asked.

The pleasing memory of how she got her name disappeared. Her gaze veered off him, a sudden interest in her meal meant to disguise the mingled anger and anguish that flashed through her each time she thought of the father who'd chosen to ignore her existence.

'I didn't have the privilege of meeting my father for the first decade and half of my life. He decided to do a runner after being with my mother for one night,' she said. 'When she found out she was pregnant and eventually tracked him down, it turned out he'd lied about his single status. And, surprise, he wasn't interested in the child he'd helped conceive.'

An expression passed over Ramon's face, almost curiously resembling fury. Although why he should be furious on her behalf was puzzling. Or maybe it was directed at her?

'And you've never sought him out all these years?'

'Not in the past ten years, no. I attempted to when

I was sixteen. I skipped school one day and went to his office. Perhaps it wasn't the best place to confront him, but what the heck do I know? Anyway, he didn't want to know me. He made it clear he wasn't interested in engaging with me on any level. So I drew a line under that.'

'Perhaps things might be different now.'

'Perhaps. But he knows where I am. He's always known where I was. He's not been inclined to seek me out. That says it all, really.'

His expression turned inward. A little bleak. A lot serious. Again his mouth tightened with a hint of fury. 'Such a waste.'

Something moved in her throat. Her hand found the back of his before she'd fully registered the move. He gave a sharp exhalation, his gaze dropping down to their touching hands before returning to her face.

'Don't take this the wrong way. Your family was a close-knit one so you may think my not knowing my father was a waste, but I don't think I missed a great deal by not having him around,' Suki said.

He tensed, his eyes narrowing on her face.

Suki bit her lip as the powder keg of the subject of denied father threatened to blow up again. 'I don't believe that about everyone, Ramon, only my own. From the little I saw of him, he and my mother would never have been compatible in the long run. I think she fell in love with the idea of falling in love more than anything. And he, of course, would never have left his wife for a one-night stand.'

'Are you saying that knowledge didn't in any way inform your own actions?' he pressed. His tone wasn't as harsh and condemning as it had been on the day of the memorial. As unyielding as the question was, this time it was powered more by the subtle need for assurance and thin layer of vulnerability than anything else.

But still she drew her hand away before she answered. 'Think about it, Ramon. We had a one-night stand too and, as you reminded me, we didn't even like each other much. But would I be here, trying to have another child with you, if I didn't want this? The doctors reassured me that the likelihood of the congenital heart failure reoccurring was low, but it's still scary—'

'*Perdón?* The what?' He cut across her, his voice a deadly blade.

Her breath strangled. 'The baby—'

'*Our* baby.'

She nodded jerkily. 'Our baby was diagnosed with congenital heart disease.' She frowned.

'You said you had me investigated. I thought you knew…'

Her words trailed off as his glass dropped onto the table, spreading red wine on the white cloth. *'Dios mio,'* he muttered through lips gone ashen. He stared at her for an infinite moment, then he jerked to his feet, paced away from the table.

'Ramon…'

He swerved back around. 'Tell me what…how…' He stopped, swallowed.

Pain shook her from scalp to toes. 'We used protection so I didn't suspect I was pregnant…for a while. I was still spotting. Anyway, when I eventually had the scan, it showed the defect, I was told the chances of her living through the very risky surgery were appallingly low. I did *extensive* research. No one could guarantee success.'

'That's why you terminated the pregnancy?'

Brokenly, she nodded.

'So you intended to keep it all along?' he pressed.

'*Yes.* You really didn't know?'

He exhaled loudly. Then his face contorted in a pained grimace. 'No. After Luis told me you'd terminated the pregnancy, I didn't have much room to hear anything else. I admit I didn't treat the messenger very well. We didn't speak for a few weeks, and, when we did, we chose not to discuss it further. My investigation was to verify time and dates and your finances, not *why* you'd terminated...' He shut his eyes and shook his head. *'Madre di Dios.'*

'I'm sorry.'

His eyes opened, spearing her with fierce remorse. 'No, I am the one who is sorry. *Lo siento mucho,*' he repeated solemnly in Spanish.

A stone lodged in her throat, and her eyes prickled. Muttering another curse, he came and crouched before her chair, his thumb brushing her tears. 'This time we will succeed,' he rasped harshly. Whether it was a command to the cosmos or a plea couched in typical Ramon arrogance, she found herself nodding, adding her own silent prayer to the statement.

He caught her hand, drew her up and walked her to the terrace. His tone subdued, he probed her gently for more information, which she freely gave, finding the sharing of the pain she'd carried for ever a little easier to bear.

An eternity later, they returned to the table. Their dinner dishes had been cleared, and the table was now set with dessert.

Ramon offered her a plate of *pastelitos* and *yemitas*. 'Eat, they're your favourite,' he instructed before heaping ice cream onto the side of the dessert bowl.

She stared at the large, mouth-watering dish. 'You're trying to fatten me up.'

'No, I'm trying to get this meal over as quickly as possible so I can drag you to the bedroom and get that damned dress off you,' he returned gruffly, stormy eyes ablaze with lust and a large dose of regret pinning hers.

He stayed true to his word. Except the dress didn't survive the inferno of his lust. Suki suspected he'd intended to rip the dress to shreds all along and didn't mourn the loss for too long. They were too busy mourning, and then reaffirming life.

But as she scooped the ripped material off the floor the next day, her mind tripped back to the night before and the disturbing subject she'd left untouched.

Svetlana. And why Ramon had lied about having broken his engagement with her. Although Luis had informed her without prompting the last time she'd seen him that Ramon and Svetlana were no longer together, the thought that he'd still been with her when he'd slept with Suki had triggered a fresh bout of bitterness.

It still did. Her fingers gripped the tattered material harder as the admission lanced her.

Why?

Because she wanted to be able to trust the father of her child completely? She didn't doubt that Ramon would be fully committed to his child. Family held a premium place in his priorities. Perhaps even the ultimate.

So why did she need other assurances that didn't...*shouldn't* matter to their agreement? Because her child would one day look up to his father and find him wanting, just as she'd found her father wanting.

Even before she fed herself that answer, Suki knew it wasn't the complete truth. She wanted to know *for herself.*

'I'm one hundred per cent sure that dress is out of commission for ever. Glaring at it quite so intensely isn't really necessary.'

She whirled around. He stood in the doorway to their—*his*—suite, the fists he'd thrust into stone-coloured chinos making his well-developed biceps, left visible by his short-sleeved V-necked shirt, bunch in eye-catching glory. A trace of tension stiffened his shoulders, and lingered in his eyes. Clearly, some of last night's subjects bothered him too.

She dragged her gaze from the spectacular sight he made to the torn dress in her hand. 'Yes... I was about to dispose of it.'

'After delivering its last rites?' he teased.

She shook her head, the alarming direction her thoughts seemed intent on taking preventing any humour from filtering through. 'No.'

His face turned serious. Striding forward, he caught her chin in his hand and tilted her face up to his. 'What's wrong?'

She started to shake her head, unsure of where this conversation would go if she started it.

He stopped her. 'Tell me, Suki.' The even tone of his voice didn't diminish the implacable demand.

'Why did you lie to me about your engagement being over the night of my birthday?' she blurted.

His whole body froze, his jaw tightening as his teeth clenched. 'I didn't lie to you,' he bit out after several tense seconds.

Her heart squeezed with disappointment far too acute for her to fool herself into thinking this conversation didn't have rippling repercussions for her emotional state. 'What does that mean? Things weren't over with her though, were they? You didn't deny that you were photographed together after you and I were...'

'Together? No, I don't deny it. And yes, she was still in my life, but we were not engaged.'

Pain she had no right to feel lanced her. But she fought to keep it from showing. 'That's just semantics, Ramon. Whether you were engaged or not, you were with her when you were with me. You weren't just a cheater, you also made me a cheater!'

His head went back at the hot accusation. His hand dropped, leaving her cold, far colder than common sense warranted she should be.

And yet the shiver that went through her was so strong, she rubbed frantic hands up and down her arms as she watched him walk away. When he reached the French doors, he turned around to face her. The look on his face was chillingly forbidding.

'That day, your birthday... I found out that she was cheating on me.'

Her gasp fell into the wide chasm that had sprung up between them. Whether he heard her or not, she wasn't sure as he continued.

'When I confronted her, she swore that it wasn't true. I didn't believe her so I ended it.'

'That's why you were in such a foul mood that night?'

He scowled at the carpet for a moment. 'That's why I jumped to conclusions about you that I shouldn't have.'

The admission salved a little, but there were gaps she needed filled. 'Right. Okay...'

'A few weeks after you, she begged me to give her the benefit of the doubt. I refused. But she had a debut movie coming up and she pleaded with me to maintain appearances until the premiere. Her morals turned out to be questionable but I didn't see the benefit in ruining her so I agreed. Besides, it also got the press off my back for a while.'

'So you maintained a relationship just for appearances' sake?' Suki wasn't sure how she felt about that.

He shrugged. 'We'd been together a year but we both led busy lives and hadn't seen each other more than a handful of times those last two months. Turning up for a three-hour premiere in exchange for a quiet exit to the relationship seemed like a good bargain.'

She frowned in remembrance. 'But that wasn't the end, was it? There were more pictures of the two of you. Even Luis believed you were still together.' She was aware she was coming across like a rabid stalker who had tracked his every move. But she couldn't stop the questions that spilled out. Or the need to understand.

'She tried to get me back after that. She refused to take off the engagement ring and turned up at a few places she knew I would be.'

'But you sent her packing?' she asked, with a lot more hope than she knew was wise.

Ramon's expression didn't alter, but his silence

told her he was weighing his words. 'She continued to plead her innocence. When she proved an
allegation false, I decided to hear her out.'

Because he'd been in love with her.

'Because you…cared about her?'

A frown twitched between his brows. 'We were
engaged to be married. Of course I cared.'

The hollow sensation in her gut shortened her
breath. 'Then why aren't you with her now?'

His face twisted in a grimace of deep bitterness
and unforgiving reprehension. 'Because only *one*
of the allegations was untrue,' he answered in an
icy voice.

When the penny dropped, her mouth gaped. 'She
cheated on you with different men?'

His jaw worked for several seconds. 'Apparently,
she was lonely and I wasn't there for her enough
so, yes, she turned to other men while convinc-
ing herself that I would be okay with it.' Impatient
fingers charged through his hair, ruffling the jet
waves. 'Are we done with the questioning, Suki?
Are you satisfied that I didn't make a cheater out
of you the night we slept together?' he asked.

Although she managed to convince herself that
the part of her that had felt battered and wronged
was appeased, the sinking sensation in the pit of
her stomach presented an even greater problem.

'Yes, I'm satisfied,' she murmured.

He exhaled, his stride steady and assured as he retraced his steps back to her. 'I came up here to tell you lunch is ready. Teresa has made *boliche*.'

For the first time since she'd started sampling his housekeeper's incredible dishes, Suki couldn't summon the appetite for the delicious Cuban pot roast. She pushed her food around her plate, forcing down bites for the sake of eating rather than enjoyment.

Also for the first time, Ramon didn't complain, his own thoughts seemingly turned inwards as the meal progressed. When another furtive glance showed his gaze in the middle distance, Suki had to bite her tongue to stop herself from asking what he was thinking of. *Who* he was thinking of.

The idea that she'd opened a vault of memories for him sat like a heavy weight on her chest. One she could no longer bear by the time their plates were cleared away.

'Do you mind if I skip dessert? I want to go for a swim in a little while and I'd rather not fall asleep in the pool.'

'If you wish,' he said, his usual droll response patently absent.

When he failed to deliver the narrow-eyed warning for her to be careful at the pool, Suki walked away from the table, the weight sitting heavier on her chest.

It stayed with her as she traversed the hallways to the room where the decorators were beginning to re-plaster the walls in readiness to replace the centuries-old carved stone that had been removed. After a short discussion with the foreman, she made her way to her suite.

The light tan she'd acquired gave her the confidence to don the canary-yellow bikini she would normally have avoided as being too eye-catching for her pasty skin. But the way she looked was the last thing on her mind as she stepped out onto the terrace and headed for the pool.

Submerging herself beneath the cool water did nothing to erase the image of Ramon's face as he spoke of Svetlana. The bitterness. The pain.

Acrid jealousy rose to choke her as his words joined in her torment.

We were engaged to be married. Of course I cared.

Did he still care? Was he still so in love with her it'd stunted his artistic passion?

She burst from beneath the water, her breath coming in pants as she clung to the edge of the pool. What was wrong with her that she couldn't get off the subject? Who Ramon cared about shouldn't feature anywhere on her emotional land-scape. What she should be giving thanks for was that her integrity hadn't been compromised.

She hadn't inadvertently stolen another wom-an's man, even if it'd been for a single unforget-table night.

And yet, she continued to cling to the tiles, her mind tripping forward to the nights she would soon *not* have. To the time when she would be relegated to sleeping alone, should her job of conceiving suc-ceed sooner rather than later.

Deep in her heart, she knew it would be sooner. But the joy of that knowledge was crushed beneath the boulder sitting on her chest.

Ramon emerged from the salon and for a mo-ment the weight lightened. Her gaze met his as he joined her at the poolside, her senses barely reg-istering the kitchen staff who followed a moment later with a tray holding fruit punch.

Ramon too had changed into a lighter T-shirt that hugged his impressive torso and a pair of swim shorts that framed his powerful thighs.

Tall, proud, virile and impossibly handsome.

His gaze obscured by aviator sunglasses, he stretched out on a lounger. She stared, unable to help herself, unable to fathom why the sight of him did such unimaginably crazy things to her. Why, even when he was with her, a part of her mourned the future loss.

How can you mourn something that never truly belonged to you?

Because she was only borrowing for a while, wasn't she?

Frustration and confusion battling through her, she pushed away from the wall, dived under the water in the vain hope that the exercise would bring her some clarity.

It didn't.

When she eventually gave up and walked up the shallow steps, he met her at the edge of the pool, wrapping a towel around her before leading her back to the loungers.

He waited until she'd patted herself dry, then poured her a drink. Thirstily, she drank the punch, eyeing him as he grabbed sun protection, squeezed a portion into his palm and tugged her foot into his lap. In silence he massaged the protection over her ankles and up her calves.

Her breath hitched when he slid those sure hands over her thighs, but, although his movements were firm and efficient, his touch didn't linger.

Fighting the hunger that was never far off when he touched her like this, she took a deep breath.

'I'm sorry if I brought back memories for you earlier.'

A handful of seconds passed, then he shrugged. *'No es nada,'* he dismissed. 'Your peace of mind is more important than my past liaisons.'

'Is it? I guess we're making progress, then.'

With the shades obscuring his eyes, she couldn't tell their expression. But she felt tension bouncing off him as his hands froze on her thigh. 'Is there something else on your mind, Suki? I thought we were done, but perhaps you wish to air whatever troubles had you clinging so tightly to the pool tiles ten minutes ago?' His voice was even, but it held the barest hint of a storm that intensified her floundering.

'You were watching me?'

'You decided you wanted to swim directly after lunch,' he replied, as if that explained everything.

'You know that those theories about cramps from swimming after a meal have been proven groundless, right?' she snapped.

'I know that you seem to be spoiling for a fight. Are you?'

The laughter that emerged was dry. 'I don't know. Maybe let's blame the past few hours on crazy hormones.' Words that were meant to be offhand suddenly grew leaden, dropped like anchors between them.

Ramon went completely still. Suki was sure he'd stopped breathing. 'To which type of hormones are you referring?' he asked, that storm powered by a different kind of energy now.

'Which do you think?' Her voice was little more than hushed sound, her instincts clamouring.

He reached up and slid off his glasses, as if he wanted no barrier between them when he asked, 'Are you sure?' His accent was pronounced; a deep husk throbbing with a maelstrom of emotions.

Suki willed her racing heart to calm. 'I... I think so.'

He stood and held out his hand in silent command. 'There's only one way to find out. Come.'

Her head tilted higher to read his face. 'Where are we going?'

'Upstairs. Unless you wish to perform the tests down here?'

Her eyes widened. 'You bought pregnancy tests?'

'*Sí*, of course. A dozen of them when we were in Miami.'

'But you didn't say anything...'

His hand extended again impatiently. 'I was waiting for you. And now you're wasting time, Suki.'

She slid her hand into his, secretly grateful for the support when she rose on shaky legs.

For a moment, they faced each other, saying nothing as hardly a breath passed between them. Then he was leading her away from the pool, through the salon and down the endless hallways to the grand staircase.

His fingers tightened around hers for a second before he made an impatient sound. The next instant, he swept her into his arms. Her already non-existent breath completely evaporated at the sizzling skin-to-skin contact. But while her senses went into free fall, he was taking the stairs with quick, purposeful strides, barely exerting himself as he carried her into his suite.

In his large, luxuriously appointed bathroom, he set her down on the cushioned vanity seat, pulled open a drawer and scooped out the long, rectangular boxes. With uncharacteristically unsteady movements, he started to rip open the boxes.

Suki stopped him when he reached for the fifth one.

'I think we have enough.'

He paused, looked as if he wanted to disagree, then gave a tight nod. 'Do you need anything else?' he rasped, casting a searching look around the bathroom.

'N-no. I'm fine.'

Still he hesitated. Finally, he nodded again, and left the bathroom.

Heart in her throat, Suki reached for the first white and blue stick. The handful of kits he'd bought were far superior quality to the ones she'd used previously, but the basics were the same.

An excruciating three minutes later, she had her answer.

She emerged to find him pacing the bedroom in tight circles, one hand clamped on his nape. He spun around immediately.

A vein throbbed at his temple. Eyes ablaze with rabid, expectant light fixed on her. His mouth worked, but no sound emerged.

The equally soul-shaking cocktail of emotions rampaging through her weakened her limbs. Leaning against the door frame, she slowly held up the sticks. 'I'm… I'm pregnant.'

His hand dropped from his neck, his eyes turning a dark, dark green she was associating with deep emotional upheaval. When after a full minute he said nothing, she nervously licked her lips. 'Did you hear—?'

'*Sí, querida.* I heard you,' he croaked.

'And?' The blend of joy, hope and naked fear in her voice was very easy to discern.

Coming to life again, he ate up the distance between them and cupped her face in his hands. She'd
seen a ruthlessly determined Ramon more times
than she cared for. The expression that crossed
his face was nothing short of a man on a crusade.

'And this time things will be different. We will
succeed this time.' He repeated the words he'd said
last night.

And because she needed that assurance more
than she would've thought possible, because she
wanted to hold on to something…anything that
affirmed the belief that things would be different
this time, she took a deep breath, and, just like last
time, she nodded. 'Yes.'

CHAPTER TEN

RAMON ENTERED THE sunlit space that was his studio one week later and drew to a stop.

The temperature was the same as it had been yesterday, the blue sky visible through his glass roof just as cloudless. The floor bore evidence of his deep frustrations. And yet, the light was almost blinding. And he felt more invigorated than he had in…hell, he couldn't remember.

Sure, there were a million other emotions bubbling beneath the surface of his skin that he didn't want to name, never mind examine, but the energy surging through him was so overwhelming, he experienced its sizzle to the very tips of his fingers.

A father. He was going to become *a father.*

He'd plotted, planned and executed it. But he hadn't allowed himself to fully embrace its possibilities. Same as he had never thought himself particularly invested in evolution or been hell-bent on leaving his mark on the Earth the way some men were obsessed with. Not until Luis had dropped the news of his lost unborn child in his lap. Not until precarious conditions on a rainy night in Mexico had caused a lorry to smash into his parents' car, ending the lives of the three people who meant the world to him.

The dark gloom and relentless anguish that dogged his days hadn't suddenly lifted, but for the first time in a long time Ramon was able to take a breath that wasn't drawn from a place of complete despair.

He knew part of that stemmed from what Suki had told him. She'd wanted their child. Fate had forced her to make a different, harrowing decision. One he couldn't fault her for. Absurdly, mourning for his lost child too now felt a little easier.

He took another deep, soul-restoring breath. He wasn't naive to the risks involved in every pregnancy, had probably over-educated himself on the subject. But the unfamiliar sentiment he first witnessed in Suki's face and was beginning to entertain himself—*hope*—had been bolstered by the requisite doctors' tests and reassurance.

All of which had turned him into the very laughable, very unrecognisable cliché of a *reborn* man.

Fairly certain it was that same alien sentiment that was leading him to re-examine other ideas he'd sealed in the *never again* vault, he'd left a napping Suki in her suite and retreated to the studio.

He looked around him at the half-finished works that had documented his turbulent state of mind.

Pieces he'd promised to his galleries for fast-approaching exhibits lay abandoned, giant hunks of metal, stone and marble enshrouded beneath black cloth.

Ignoring them, he crossed the cavernous space to the back of the studio where untouched slabs of stone and marble were lined up on wheel brackets. Running his hands over the raw material, he settled on the smooth Carrara marble.

Wheeling it to the middle of the room, he yanked off his T-shirt, powered up his tools and started to sculpt.

Three hours later, the frame of his idea had begun to take shape. Unsettlingly, so had the idea that the parameters of the bargain he'd struck with Suki could...*should* be altered.

Like the master strategist the world claimed him to be, he stepped back from fully embracing it, weighing the pros and cons as the days passed.

In many ways it wasn't a road he wanted to go down again. But there was more than himself to think about now. And his child outweighed any con that stood in his way.

So he chipped away, until the one that remained was Suki herself.

The first six weeks of pregnancy rolled by in a dizzying tumult of blinding joy, hopefulness and inevitable moments of abject fear. The urge to make plans, choose a nursery and start decorating immediately was tempered by the need to exercise brutal caution. With each day that passed, Suki counted her blessings. Hell, she even welcomed the double bout of morning sickness that plagued her this time round.

Through it all, Ramon remained a steady presence at hand to see to her general well-being. Just as he'd made it his mission to get her pregnant, he took on the role of ruthless overseer with aplomb, never straying far when she was awake, reciting bare but reassuring statistics when worry threatened to take over.

He found excuses to be in the room when she tested colour swatches on walls and supervised the staining of the new mantelpiece. He threw a casual arm over her shoulder and held her at a distance when the restorers reinserted the mosaic windows and even helped her re-plaster the priceless tiles.

The belief that he would be committed to his child was indelibly cemented into place. Between that, the doctors' continued reassurance about her healthy pregnancy and the fact that her mother had undergone the first round of treatment and come through with flying colours should've placed her somewhere on cloud nine.

Except for one large hole in the fabric of her contentment.

She and Ramon no longer shared a bed. Despite knowing the day was coming, his immediate and complete withdrawal following confirmation of her pregnancy had lodged a nasty little ball of anguish in her chest she hadn't been able to destroy no matter how much she tried.

And she'd tried.

By reminding herself how her presence here came about. By summoning up Svetlana's drop-dead gorgeous form, comparing it to her own and reiterating that she would always be found wanting.

And if that wasn't enough, she had Ramon's own words to remind her why she needed to find a way to deal with the silly torment of her crush.

We were engaged to be married. Of course I cared...

Except Suki couldn't hide from the fact that this

time, it was more than a crush. Her crush had been unwieldy and inconvenient. So much so she'd given in at the first true lesson in temptation in the hope of getting rid of it.

But this...

This ache grew mockingly bigger, churning more anguish with each passing day. And it stemmed from the simple knowledge that she missed him. Missed his sometimes acerbic tongue. Missed him teasing her about her love of Teresa's cooking.

Most of all, she missed falling asleep in his arms. A fact she readily accepted was her most foolish yearning of all.

'What's wrong?'

She jumped at the sharp demand, her heart racing as her hand stilled from the light gloss she'd been applying to the frame of an antique painting that had once hung in the drawing room that was being restored.

Carefully she modulated her voice so her feelings wouldn't bleed through. 'What do you mean? Nothing's wrong.'

'Then why were you standing there with your face contorted and your hand on your stomach?' came the sharper query.

Realising the direction of his thoughts, she dropped the rag, set the painting against the wall, and turned. 'Ramon, there's nothing wrong, I prom—' The rest of the words died in her throat at the sight of him.

He was shirtless. Again. A light sheen of sweat covered his insanely chiselled torso and dampened the trail of hair disappearing beneath the waistband of weathered trousers that were stained with specks of marble dust and the special oil he used on his tools when he was sculpting.

Suki wanted to blame pregnancy hormones for the way her senses went into meltdown at the sight of his half-naked form, but she knew that would be false. Her stupefying reaction to Ramon was nothing new. But it would seriously get out of hand if she wasn't careful.

'You were saying?' he pressed, one hand reaching into his back pocket to pluck a towel to wipe his grimy fingers on.

The sight of those slim, capable fingers, the sweat on his skin, the earthy, sexy smell of him.

Dear God, he was too much.

'I was saying I'm fine,' she replied, her voice waspish. 'And do you have to go around half naked all the time?'

One eyebrow spiked. 'Does the sight of me offend you?' he drawled.

She wanted to laugh. And cry. Maybe throw in

a scream or two. Instead, she chose the high road paved with composure and dignity. 'On second thought, forget it. It's your house. You can come and go as you please, I suppose.'

'*Gracias*... I think,' he returned dryly.

With nothing more to add, and the even more urgent need to do something other than give in to the temptation to stare at his glorious half-nakedness, she picked up the painting and started walking towards the door. She'd barely taken a few steps when he intercepted her and took it from her.

'I hired an additional team so you didn't have to do your own carrying, Suki,' he grumbled.

Once her morning sickness had abated, a second team of architects had arrived. With the detailed photos from the room, they'd come up with a schedule of when the restoration works would start. She'd been forbidden from any lifting so Suki set up a temporary office in one of the many bedrooms on the second floor and contented herself with choosing the antique furniture, wallpaper and drapes to finish the room with once the work was done.

'That painting weighs less than my laptop and, besides, I need the exercise.'

His scowl was pure storm clouds. 'Not one that

involves you going up and down the stairs a dozen times a day.'

She stopped herself from pointing out that she'd only been down twice today, both times at his bidding, to share a meal with him. 'Was there a particular reason you came looking for me? Or are you gracing me with your grumpy presence just for laughs?'

He paused at the top of the stairs and eyed her. 'Now who's grumpy?'

'You haven't answered my questions.'

He observed her pursed-lips response for a minute before he started walking down the stairs.

Following a step behind him, she couldn't avoid staring at his gladiator-like physique, the beautiful musculature of his back and the light bounce of his slightly unruly hair as he moved in that deeply animalistic way unique to him.

One of the restorers was coming out of a hallway as they reached the ground floor. Ramon handed over the painting with a flurry of Spanish that received several quick and agreeable nods, before he turned to her.

'Let's go.'

'Go where? And what did you say to the contractor?' she asked.

He turned in the direction of the main salon and

she, with no choice, followed. 'I suggested that perhaps they would be better off making less trips to the kitchen to take advantage of our housekeeper's culinary skills and more manpower keeping you from having to traipse around with antiques. He was kind enough to agree.'

'Ramon!'

He stopped, turned to face her. And she noticed that, despite his casual tone, he was highly vexed. 'We had a deal, *guapa*. One that I'd hoped wouldn't need us to have this conversation.'

'You're overreacting.'

He stepped closer, bringing more of that irritated, hard-packed body into her personal space. 'Am I?' he enquired softly, his gaze raking her face before it locked on her mouth.

'Yes, you are,' she said. And then because she lived with the same fear every single second, she cleared her throat. 'But I have it on good authority, they will be done before the end of the week, so they will be out of your hair.'

His eyes didn't move from her mouth. '*Bene*. I will not have to tear my hair out after all.'

Her gaze tracked to his full head of vibrant hair. 'You can spare a few, I'm sure. And seeing as I've saved your mane, maybe you will start wearing a shirt?' she asked, hoping her tone was less pleading and more irritated.

Green eyes flicked up to meet hers. Then a low deep laugh rumbled up from his throat. Unfettered. Sexy. Spellbinding. The sound, rarely heard and not at all recently, wrapped around her. It only lasted a handful of seconds but every cell in her body lifted, strained towards the incredible sound.

'You agree to no more carrying heavy stuff around and I'll think about it,' he replied.

'Okay, fine. I agree.'

He muttered something Spanish under his breath before resuming his stride down the hallway. When they reached the salon, he held the door open for her. The sun-drenched beauty of the room never failed to soothe her. She walked around, trailing her fingers over priceless antique furniture steeped in history.

Ramon stayed at the entrance of the salon, leaning against the door frame and studying her for a long moment. When his scrutiny got too much, she dropped her hand from the bronze bust she'd been examining. 'Is there any reason you're staring at me like that?'

'I've started working on the first piece he made me promise to do for you,' he said, his voice containing a solemn tone that made her heart kick.

'He…you mean Luis?'

Ramon nodded. 'Yes.'

'You're sculpting and painting again.'

His face was unreadable. '*Sí*, it seems I am.'

Suki wanted to ask how…when…*why*? Too scared of the answer, she ventured softly instead, 'I…am I allowed to know what it is?'

'It's a sculpture. But I haven't decided what it'll be yet. I sketched out a few ideas. But I need a live representation. I choose you.'

Shock slayed her. 'Me?'

'To be the subject, *sí*.'

A shiver went through her. There was something viscerally exposing about what he was asking. 'I'm not…are you—?'

'Don't think up excuses.'

'I wasn't. I was just going to ask if you were sure.'

He shrugged. 'I have tried several inanimate objects. They're not working. You are the most convenient living test subject.'

'Wow, suddenly I don't feel so special,' she muttered.

A heavy and bleak expression fleeted through his eyes. 'You were special to him. I should've considered you first and saved myself much wasted time.'

Her hurt abated a little even though she knew

she would need a scalpel to dig out the precious meaning hidden in his words.

'Will you do it?' he rasped.

It would be a gift from her best friend from beyond the grave. One she could cherish for ever. 'Yes, of course I will.'

He gestured her forward. 'Good. Let's go.'

She looked down at the white cotton, short-sleeved tunic she'd thrown on hastily this morning to meet the restorers. Beneath it, she wore the canary-yellow bikini that had fast become her favourite swimsuit. 'Do I need to change?'

He conducted a long scrutiny from loose hair to sandalled feet. 'No, you're fine as you are.'

They left the villa by way of a little-used hallway at the back of the villa. Like everywhere in the villa and on the grounds, the winding stone path dissecting the back garden and leading to Ramon's brick and glass studio was immaculately kept. He punched in a code and the sturdy double doors sprang ajar.

Her preconceived idea of what Ramon's artist's studio would look like was smashed to smithereens the second she walked in. He'd cleaned up the carnage, obviously, but still, expecting the stereotypical, paint-splattered chaos of a passionate artist's creative space, she froze to a halt at what confronted her.

On either side of the whitewashed walls, rows of tall and short objects were covered with black cloth. And on the long bench that held dozens of pots of paint and brushes, each one was laid out at a precise angle.

The floor beneath her feet had been painted a pristine white too, the light pouring in from the windows giving the space an almost other-worldly dimension.

A dimension where everything was set in its place. Almost chastely so.

Everything except the raised platform at the end of the space and the single black armchair that served as an observation point for the platform. On the floor next to the chair, a half-empty bottle of dark rum stood next to a crystal tumbler containing dregs of amber liquid.

As if that weren't awe-inspiring enough, her gaze rose higher, her eyes widening as she walked further forward to better see the untouched slab of solid black granite suspended from the ceiling.

Against the white walls and floor, the platform and the piece that would form a stunning sculpture one day was wildly hypnotic, commanding and receiving attention. Suki stopped behind the chair, unable to take her eyes off it.

The mental vision of Ramon watching that piece of stone, sketching, viscerally connecting with his subject…his muse…breathing life into the piece was so visually mesmerising, she didn't hear him speak above the growing buzzing in her blood.

'Suki?'

She snatched a quick, restorative breath and faced him. 'Yes?'

'Are you okay?'

She nodded quickly, dragging her gaze from the spectacle before her. 'I'm fine. Umm…why is everything covered?' she asked, hoping to cover her flustered senses.

'I don't like distractions when I work.'

Distractions or *reminders*?

Unbidden, the memory of how Ramon and Svetlana had met rose to her mind. According to Luis, he'd seen her on a catwalk in Milan and had been so struck with her, he'd asked to paint her. Within days they were lovers. Before their first month was over, he'd asked her to marry him.

Emotion she recognised as naked jealousy spiked through her blood. 'Do you have other studios?' she blurted before she could stop herself.

The unexpected question drew a frown. 'No, this is my only one. Why?'

So he'd brought Svetlana here. Painted and sculpted her here. Suki shook her head, swallowing down the sick feeling that surged high. 'I'm just…curious.'

He continued to stare at her for probing seconds. Unable to stand it, she turned around, walked closer to the steps leading up to the platform. This time the noise in her ears was the creaky churning of her heart. And again she didn't hear him when he addressed her.

'I'm sorry, what did you say?'

He prowled to the edge of the platform, stared down at her with narrowed eyes. 'I said, take off your dress.'

Her heart skidded, then jumped into her throat as heat engulfed her. 'I…what?

'The dress, Suki. Take it off. Then lie down on there.' He indicated behind her with his chin.

Turning, she saw that the slab had somehow been lowered to hip level. From where she stood it looked like a narrow bed. A bed from which would be hewn a magnificent piece of art from Ramon's hands. The same hands that had thrilled her so thoroughly when they'd made love.

Sizzling heat flowed over her body, singeing the

apex of her thighs and tightening her nipples in remembered torment. Crossing her arms in front of her to hide her body's weakness, she slipped off her thongs and climbed up the three shallow steps of the platform. Behind her, Ramon tracked her movements, towering over her as she slowly reached out to touch the stone.

There was no give in the chains holding it in place.

'Don't be concerned—it will hold your weight.'

She wanted to say that wasn't her concern. She wanted to say she didn't want to lie down because she was afraid of what she would reveal from being this close to something so powerful. Of what he'd see when she was exposed to him.

And she would be. Ramon had been right when he recounted Luis's imitation of her the one time they visited Piedra Galleries in London. Every single one of Ramon's pieces of work had held her in thrall. Touching his pieces had been like touching the man himself.

And that was even before she'd shared his bed, taken him into her body. Been impregnated with his child. Now the sensation was ten times more potent. Because all those feelings were beginning to take a certain shape, make a terrifying kind of sense.

Sensing her prevarication, he stepped closer.

'Now, Suki,' he commanded huskily from behind her.

She wanted to refuse. But, of course, she didn't.
Because the slavish compulsion to give him what
he wanted also made a terrifying kind of sense.

She caught the hem of her tunic, her hands effi-
ciently tugging the flimsy material over her head.

His harsh exhalation echoed through the space
as he caught the dress from her weak fingers and
flung it away.

'Now the rest,' he instructed thickly.

Her breath strangled in her lungs but refusal
never crossed her mind. Fingers shaking, she
tugged the strings of the bikini top and bottom
free until they fell away, until she stood naked,
her head bowed, her tumbling hair flowing over
her shoulders.

Slowly, she sensed him circling her, tracking her
every shiver, her every breath.

When he stopped directly in front of her, she
raised her head, met his gaze straight on.

Saw for herself that he too was affected.

Hectic colour tinged taut cheekbones, his bare
chest rising and falling in ragged breathing. Both
hands came up and wrapped around the chains se-

curing the slab, his knuckles showing white as his red-hot gaze flew over her body.

'Lie down, Suki.' Again the instruction was thick, his voice barely discernible.

Two short steps brought her to the raw ingredient that would form his masterpiece. Reaching out, she touched it, familiarised herself with its texture. Lowering herself onto it, she stretched out on her back. The heat of her body meeting the cold drew a shiver and a gasp from her.

Ramon stared down at her, her feet a scant inch from his powerful thighs and the potent reaction to her that currently bulged behind his zipper. Suki wasn't sure whether it was the fire from his gaze or the blaze from her body that soon warmed the stone beneath her.

Ferocious need clamouring through her, she couldn't stop the sinuous movement of her body or the hand that slid over her midriff to rest on her belly.

Although she'd gained weight in the last several weeks, her stomach had remained flat. And yet she felt different, her not-yet-visible pregnancy powering a change she felt from head to toe.

Now, as Ramon's eyes lingered at the place where their child grew, a tumult of emotions wove over his face.

'*Dios mio,*' he breathed as his gaze raked over her, absorbed the subtle changes in her body.

After a long minute, he lurched away from the slab. Going to the long workbench, he grabbed a large sketchpad and a thin wedge of grey charcoal. Returning, he threw himself into the chair, poured a finger of rum and knocked it back.

Then his hand began to fly over the surface of the pad.

Time sped up. Or slowed to a crawl. She lost the ability to judge as she was caught up in a singularly transcendental experience.

When Ramon instructed her, she turned this way and that, making sure not to jar her body. Finally, he set the pad down and poured himself another drink.

Eyes gone almost black with unfathomable emotions regarded her as he rolled the tumbler between his palms.

Had she not lived through his effortless rejection of her these past few weeks, or known that everything he did was in pursuit of his heir, Suki's heart would've soared high.

But the knowledge was inescapable. And with it came an agony that drew a rough sound from her throat. Probing eyes that saw way too much shifted from where they were stalled on the rise and fall of her stomach to snag her own.

Tossing the drink back, he stood and came up the platform, caught her hand and helped her upright. 'Are you okay?' he rasped.

Attempting to speak past the sensation clogging her throat was hard, but she barely managed. 'Did you get what you needed?'

For some reason the question made him tense.

One by one, the emotions disappeared from his face and he brought himself under rigid, effortless control. Resolutely, he stepped back and left the platform, once again rejecting her. 'Yes. You can get dressed now.'

As Suki slid off the slab, retied her bikini and pulled on her tunic, her heart finally accepted the truth and tumbled into deep mourning. But even the monumental knowledge of what had happened didn't stop her from caressing the granite one last time.

Because whether or not Ramon used the sketches he'd made of her, she would associate this studio, this platform, this piece of stone with the moment she'd accepted that her stupid crush had turned into something much, much bigger for ever.

CHAPTER ELEVEN

'I THINK WE need a change of scene.'

'A change of scene to where?' Suki asked without turning around from where she was basking in the spectacular sunset. In the two weeks since he'd taken the sketches of her, she'd barely seen Ramon. Each morning after breakfast, he disappeared into his studio.

His presence at lunch and dinner had been replaced by an extra attentive Teresa, who had even attempted to learn a few English phrases in order to engage her in conversation.

As much as Suki appreciated the housekeeper's efforts her appetite had been reduced to forcing food down merely to maintain a healthy pregnancy.

She was in love with Ramon Acosta.

He was only interested in the baby she carried.

No matter how many times she told herself the latter to mitigate any further pain, her heart lurched harder, the pain growing more acute. Her hand tightened around the metal banister that edged the villa's flat roof terrace.

Suki had taken to escaping up here when the worst of the day's heat abated to enjoy the sunset, and the cast-iron bench seats with plump cushions set beneath a simple ivy-covered gazebo were the perfect place to retreat. Either with a book or with the thoughts that were determined not to leave her be.

Hearing the clatter of crockery behind her, she turned to see one of Teresa's minions was heading their way holding a tray. Suki had stopped wondering how the housekeeper knew when to strike with her snacks but then discovered there was actually a twenty-four-hour roster in the kitchen ensuring the endless supply of food.

The unexpected appearance and steady approach of the man who dominated those thoughts sent a skitter of alarm over her skin.

And equally punishing, he was once again shirtless.

She couldn't hide her reaction to the electrifying stimulus or stop the breath that caught dangerously in her midriff, all of which Ramon clocked with perceptive eyes.

'Come and sit down.' He indicated the chairs, murmuring an order to the maid before relieving her of the tray of refreshing drinks and a plate of *yemitas*.

Leaving the balcony, she took a seat on the sofa, numbly accepting a cup of decaf coffee she had no interest in drinking and a small platter of pastries.

Ramon helped himself to an espresso before he snagged one pastry for himself. Sitting back, he chewed and swallowed, his inscrutable eyes on her. 'My art foundation holds a month-long talent-sourcing contest for Cuban artists every September. It's open to twenty-five entrants. The final selection is made in mid-October and we showcase ten of them at my galleries over a two-week period.'

The unexpected subject that had nothing to do with food or vitamins piqued her interest. 'Here in Cuba?'

He nodded. 'Initially, but also in other Piedra Galleries. Teresa tells me you've stopped eating and are a whisper away from going stir crazy. Now your mother is back in London undergoing the second stage of her treatment, I think we should visit the galleries together. We can stop in London to see your mother after Madrid.'

She didn't clock the middle part of his statement immediately because she was too busy being giddy at the thought of time spent on something else other than her tormenting thoughts. Even if that time involved seeing Ramon's work again. 'That would be—wait, you've been having Teresa spy on me?' Her voice rose almost comically.

He gave an unapologetic shrug. 'She's just as invested in your welfare as I am. And I'm hoping we'll get you out of here before that situation fully blooms.'

'I'm not going stir—' She stopped as the maid returned, holding something in her hand. Rising fluidly to his feet, Ramon took it from her and returned tugging a dark sea-green T-shirt over his chest. Absurdly, even though her senses screamed at the torture of being subjected to the breathtaking masterpiece of his body, she mourned its disappearance once he covered himself up. It was probably why she was still staring at him as he returned, sat down and drained his coffee.

Setting his mug on the tray, he cocked an eyebrow at her. 'Are you happy now, *belleza*?' he drawled.

Tuning off her observation of the amazing things the colour did to his eyes, she finished her own decaf coffee. 'It's a good start,' she declared briskly.

Her senses were too jumpy to ascertain whether she caught a trace of laughter before he inclined his head. 'The first exhibition is this Friday. My assistant will put together an itinerary and put the medical team on standby.'

Her heart performed a sickening lurch. 'Do we need to take them with us?' The twice weekly visits by the team of doctors had been bearable before but were beginning to wear on her nerves.

Grim resolve crawled over his features, his body tensing in preparation for a fight. 'Yes. It's non-negotiable, Suki.'

She rose from the sofa, her agitated steps taking her back to the balcony. Below her lay the beautifully manicured gardens, carefully and attentively tended by Mario. Beyond the boundaries of the villa, the captivating port city of Cienfuegos, which had been awarded World Heritage Site status, went on as normal, unknowing that she was falling in love with its rich culture, thriving art and vintage cars, falling in love with one of its most dedicated citizens.

When she felt Ramon's approach, she turned, met the penetrating eyes that seemed to see into her soul. 'Even if their presence taunts me with the possibility that something could go wrong at any moment?' she blurted.

A tiny flash of shock sparked his eyes at her

naked admission. Then he frowned. 'I hadn't quite thought of it that way.'

Of course he hadn't. Her heart twisted painfully. 'You ran a global empire and are used to having teams troubleshoot problems sometimes before they happen. It's a natural reaction for you. It's not for me.'

He reached out and tucked a strand of hair behind her ear. Although the gesture was a gentle one, his body remained tense, his gaze calculating and direct. 'It's the most efficient way to mitigate potential problems.'

Her fists balled, but she struggled to keep her voice even. Her emotions where he was concerned might be slipping out of her control but she could control this. 'I'm not a potential business problem, Ramon.'

His hand dropped, his hands shoving into his pockets. The gaze that had hers captive swept down, shutting her out. When it rose again it was charged with double the purpose. 'No. I've lost too much. I won't risk this baby's safety.'

Pain lanced her. 'And you think I will?'

His jaw clenched tight. 'I think you should remember our agreement. You agreed to the presence of a medical team for the duration of the pregnancy. You won't go back on your promise now,' he finished harshly.

The finality of that statement, the reminder that she was just the vessel incubating his heir, hollowed out any last vestige of the hope that she foolishly clung to in the dark of night. The hope that if they'd been as compatible in bed as she recalled, then perhaps, once the baby was born, they could go forge something out of the bones of that compatibility. It'd been a shameless, desperate wish. But a wish that she'd thought had foundations.

The look in his eyes told a different story.

Chemistry might prompt his body to react a certain way to hers but the most important part of him, his heart, would never be hers.

Slowly she unfurled her fists. 'Fine. Since that's what your piece of paper states, then, by all means, have them come.'

Skirting his imposing form, she hurried away from the terrace.

Ramon watched her walk away, wondering if the tempestuous upheaval that best described his current state of being was pushing him into taking decisions that weren't entirely sound.

No, he concluded in the next breath. What was more sound than ensuring the optimal well-being of Suki and their baby? He knew the statistics. He also knew that expert care and quick action during a crisis would be the difference between saving the ones he cared about and having his heart ripped out all over again.

He couldn't take that.

But what about her fears?

Discomfort irritated beneath his skin, the voice very much like his brother's sparking a deep vexation.

She'd signed the agreement, yes, but did a piece of paper take into account the true reality? For the first time he'd allowed himself to truly hear her. Had he allowed himself to see the torment that always lurked in her eyes? The same torment she must have felt when faced with the diagnosis of their baby the first time round.

She'd lived through it. He hadn't. Did he not owe her the benefit of a little peace of mind?

But at what cost?

Gripping his nape, he looked to the heavens, seeking clarity. But as with everything else, he knew he would only find it within himself. And yet the instinct he'd trusted all of his life was flashing with an *out of order* signal. Because the options it was throwing out were laughable.

Or perhaps you don't want to trust what it's saying?

'Shut up, *hermano*,' he sneered under his breath.

Dios, he was losing his mind.

Folding his arms, he leaned against the balcony and attempted to calm his racing thoughts. But nothing would be calmed. Nothing had been calm since he first set eyes on Suki, he realised. She managed to consume his thoughts with very little effort.

Day or night.

Except he'd found a minimal outlet in the form of the nearly finished sculpture residing in his studio.

The sculpture you're tipping into obsession over?

He growled under his breath. So what if he was obsessed? He'd made a promise and he planned on keeping it. No matter that he was pouring a part of himself into the project than he'd never done before?

No matter that he fell into bed and dreamed about the subject of the project and woke up with a hollow feeling in his chest?

Suficiente.

Taking his phone from his pocket, he dialled his assistant's number, relayed precise instructions and hung up. Then he turned around, intent on taking a moment's peace of mind to enjoy the last of the blazing sunset.

Thirty seconds later, he was reaching for his phone again, and delivering slightly modified instructions.

The mocking laughter that rang in his ears, Ramon studiously decided to ignore.

Their journey to Havana two days later went without a hitch. As did the first exhibit of the talented artists who'd made the cut of his programme. The eclectic mix of local artists, avid collectors and overseas gallery owners interested in the thriving Cuban art scene meant the event was fully attended.

Already he'd fielded calls from other galleries in the States and Europe interested in featuring three of the artists.

He'd finished delivering the news to the artists in question when she caught his eye from the corner of the room. Hell, who was he kidding? His body's radar had known where she was at every single moment, even after she'd politely excused herself on arrival and made sure to put the width of the room between them from then on.

From across the room of Piedra Galleria Havana, he watched her converse with one of his artists. The short-sleeved lace dress hugged her upper arms and slim torso before flaring in a full calf-length skirt. With her hair caught up and delicate silver jewellery complementing her style, she was easily the most captivating woman in the room.

A fact evidenced by the volume of male attention directed her way.

The powerful hit of pure possessiveness didn't surprise him. Nor did the recognition that part of his irritation stemmed from the fact that her full skirt prevented him from seeing her belly. He didn't care that her pregnancy wasn't outwardly visible yet.

The caveman in him wanted his claim on her in plain sight.

Mine, he wanted to growl. But the word stayed locked in his throat. Because to utter that, he would need another word to give truth to the situation. *Temporarily.*

So the claim stayed down, and he watched as she nodded eagerly in conversation, then replied. The young artist, clearly thrilled to have a captive audience, proceeded to elaborate whatever point he was making with animated hand gestures. Ramon watched a smile break over her face, the first he'd seen for a while. The knot in his stomach annoyed him almost as much as the ever-closing gap between Suki and the artist.

A server approached them. Ramon watched the man snag two glasses of champagne and hand her one. Another smile accompanied her refusal, which should've made him back away. Instead, he leaned ever closer to catch what she was saying.

Ramon was moving across the floor before he'd fully registered the movement of his limbs. He reached them in time to hear his cocky cajoling.

'Come on, a simple drink for the man who put the first smile on your face tonight, *sí*?'

'When a woman states that she doesn't want a drink, you need to be a gentleman and respect her wishes,' Ramon cut in coldly.

Diego Baptiste's attention jerked his way, whatever objection he'd been about to put up dying when he saw Ramon.

He took a hasty step back, almost tripping over his feet. '*Sí, lo siento.* I did not mean any disrespect...enjoy your evening, *señorita*.' Turning on his heel, he struck a straight route into the busy crowd.

Stunning blue eyes, holding distinct accusation, glared at him. 'He was being nice. Did you have to put him down like that?'

A hovering waiter approached. Ramon chose a peach mocktail he knew she would enjoy and handed it to her, then grabbed a glass of cognac for himself, after which he walked her out of Diego's *papier-maché* exhibition into one more pleasing to him. 'He was encroaching where he had no business encroaching. So yes, the put-down was necessary.'

Her eyes snapped. 'Encroaching? We were just talking. And you're the host of this event. If you insist on glaring at everyone who walks past, don't do it in my presence.'

'You're the most beautiful woman in the room. No man wants to *just talk* to you,' he bit out. 'And I can glare at whomever I damn well please.'

She gave a dry laugh, but even that sound attracted more stares. 'What's got into you? If I didn't know better I'd think you were jealous.'

'Then I hate to be the bearer of bad news because you don't know any better,' he replied.

The glass in her hand wobbled. Her eyes widened adorably before heat flared up into her face along with a healthy measure of the confusion firing through his own bloodstream. 'Ramon...'

'You look stunning, *querida*, but I hate that dress you're wearing.'

Her peach-glossed, deliciously kissable lips pursed. 'Blame yourself, you chose it.'

'Well, at the time I didn't know that I would crave seeing your body bloom with my baby.'

She gave a soft gasp, then her forehead creased in puzzlement. 'Are…are you okay?'

He gave a dry laugh of his own then, unable to resist, he stepped forward and slid a hand around her waist. 'No. That skirt you're wearing covers you a little too well.'

'I'm not showing yet. And can we drop the wardrobe preferences for a minute?'

Splaying his fingers on her lower back, he pulled her closer until the top of her head was just below his chin, and he was breathing in the alluring scent of her apple shampoo and heady perfume.

'I wasn't as accommodating to your concerns as I should've been two days ago.'

She tensed, but she didn't move away from him. Ramon chose to see that as a victory.

'I feel like we've been here before but this time on a much grander scale. Is this your way of apologising?' she asked.

He allowed himself a small smile. 'If I say I need time to find the right words will you ride in my limo again?'

'Been there, done that,' she quipped. 'I'm wearing the metaphorical T-shirt right now.'

His hand left her waist to catch her feisty chin in his hand. 'You wear it beautifully and bravely. And your concerns have been noted and acted upon.'

Her gaze searched his. 'Really?'

'*Sí.*'

'How?'

'Leave the logistics to me. Just rest assured that, should we need them, the doctors will be there.'

She nodded after a handful of seconds, relief lightening her eyes. 'Thank you.'

'*De nada.*'

She started to step away. He scrambled with a reason to hold her close. When no coherent ones punched through the atmosphere of his confusion, he simply splayed his hand over her belly, feeling the slight firmness where his child was beginning to establish its presence.

She froze. A light quivering transmitted through his fingers. Her lowered gaze remained on his chest. Hiding from him.

'Look at me, Suki.' He waited for her gaze to reconnect with his. 'This baby matters. But you matter equally. *Entiendes?*'

Her eyes grew bright. Then she nodded.

The tightness in his chest eased a fraction. Not enough to give him peace, but it was a start. 'Are you ready to leave?'

She glanced around, clocked the people hovering nearby. 'There are about a dozen people waiting to talk to you.'

'They're not important. Besides, every single piece sold out an hour ago and commissions are flooding in for the artists. My work here is done.' His pride in his fellow artists and the work his foundation was doing was undeniable. But right now he wanted to get out of here. Wanted to test the waters with the daunting plan that loomed larger in his brain with every passing minute.

'If you're sure?' She set her untouched drink down.

The faint shadows beneath her eyes sealed his answer. 'I'm sure. Let's go.'

He meshed his fingers through hers, kept the inevitable interaction between the room and the door to a minimum. He felt her slight hesitation as his limo pulled up.

Their interactions in the back of his limos had so far been...memorable. The hot tug of need to his groin confirmed which of the experiences he would repeat given the choice.

Helping her into the car, he slid in behind her and gave the instructions for the airport.

She glanced at him in surprise. 'We're leaving right now?'

'I thought we'd kill two birds with one stone. You're tired and need to get some sleep. I need to catch up on Acosta Hotel business before we land in Madrid. We can do both on the plane.'

And once she was awake, he would proceed.

She looked out of the window for a second before her gaze met his.

A little apprehensive. A lot alluring, with a swathe of hair falling over one eye. The urge to reach out and slide the wavy silk through his fingers raked through him. He settled for securing her seat belt as the car moved off.

Either she was too tired to protest or his idea wasn't unwelcome, but the yawn that overtook her superseded everything else. Kicking off her shoes, she rested her head against the seat. 'Okay,' she said simply, before her eyes drifted shut.

Her easy acquiescence kicked a pulse of worry down his spine that lingered all the way to the airport. Once he had confirmation that his instructions had been carried out, he allowed himself to relax a touch.

She awakened long enough to get out of the car when they arrived at his plane. Swinging her into his arms, he strode up the stairs. Felt more tension leave him again as she curled into his chest. His plan was the right one.

In his grief and anger, he'd only seen things short

term, a quick way to stop the agony of his loss. It was time to think long term.

Take-off was smooth, and they were halfway over the Atlantic by the time she woke up. From his armchair in the large cabin bedroom, he watched her sit up, push her silky hair back from her face. Warm, sleepy, beautiful, she blinked in the soft lamplight for a minute before she spotted him.

Her hand dropped from her hair, the deliberate action obscuring her face from him. Ramon forced himself to stay put. 'Did you sleep well, *belleza*?'

'I slept well.' She looked down at herself, saw the half-slip she wore and tensed. 'You undressed me?' Her voice held the guardedness he'd been subjected to in varying forms for the last two weeks.

'*Sí*, your dress was too restricting. I wanted to make you more comfortable.'

She nodded, still not looking at him. The tension he'd thought he'd talked himself out of ramped up his spine. Leaning forward on his elbows, he took a breath.

'Suki, we need to talk.'

Her slim shoulders stiffened, the square inch of coverlet caught in her fingers twisting over and over. 'So talk,' she invited. But her voice lacked warmth, her throat working as she swallowed.

Dios, this was insane.

He'd faced some of the toughest negotiators in the world and hadn't felt as nervous and out of his depth as he did right now. 'It's time to discuss our baby's future. *Our* future,' he said.

Her head snapped up, her eyes finding his. A deep, bruised wariness lurked in the blue depths and that drowning pain was back in his chest. Expanding.

'We *agreed* we would discuss it after the baby was born. That's months from now.'

He nodded. 'I know, but—'

'I won't give up my baby!' She was leaning forward, her chin jutting out in challenge as she placed one protective hand over her stomach. 'You should know that right now. It's non-negotiable. I will fight you in court for as long as I live, if need be.'

Her fierceness lit a fire in the cold, hard places in him. But that jealousy he'd felt earlier tonight reared its head. The knowledge that this time it was directed at his own child was shameful. But, *sí*, he wasn't perfect. He wanted that fierceness for himself.

'I'm not asking you to give him up. I'm asking that we join forces. That whatever platform we launch from, we do it together.'

She frowned, her fingers twisting even more

frantically. He wanted to go to her, take those hands in his. Kiss her. Tell her about every insane emotion that prowled within him. But how could he, when he didn't know it himself?

'I'm sorry, Ramon. You lost me.'

He took a deep breath and rose. Partly because he couldn't sit still any longer. Partly because he needed to be near her when he said the words. 'I want to make this permanent. I want you to marry me.'

CHAPTER TWELVE

SUKI WAS GLAD she was sitting down because she was sure his words—and the sudden bolt of turbulence that hit the plane—would've flattened her.

'What?'

He opened his mouth, but she shook her head quickly, holding up her hands, needing time to absorb what he'd said.

'It's okay, you don't need to repeat it. I heard you. What I meant was *why*?'

A look curled through his eyes and his nostrils flared as if he was gathering himself. The very deep, very real quicksand she'd been sinking in since she admitted the depths of her feelings for Ramon, threatened to suck her down even faster.

Because it was clear he was up to something.

'Our current circumstances are a strong reason to advocate marriage, are they not?'

Her heart lurched harder, and she fought ready tears that prickled her heart. 'When only a few weeks ago you fully denounced it? Your exact words were...*marriage is not for me*, if I recall correctly?' Knowing now what she didn't know then, the statement hurt even more.

He'd been betrayed by the woman he loved and had closed himself off for ever. For him to force himself back down that road...

'Things have changed. *I* have changed. And we're coming from a different place this time.'

She wanted to admire that earth-shaking sentiment. Perhaps, she even did somewhere deep within her. But the seething pain of her wrecked heart didn't give her enough room to feel magnanimous right then.

'Are we?'

He surged to his feet, moving towards her with speed that belied his overpowering presence.

'*Sí*. If we're both committed to making this work, we will succeed. I want to try.'

He stopped at the side of the bed, his green eyes blazing down at her with a light she wished with all her heart were hers to own. Hers to love. But she knew it wasn't.

All this was for his child.

Heart mourning, she shook her head. 'I... I don't think I—'

His hand shot out, stopping her answer. 'Perhaps this wasn't the best timing in the world.' He glanced at the lowered shutters then back to her. 'Proposing at thirty-seven thousand feet is unique but it wasn't what I had in mind. Don't give me your answer now. For the sake of what's at stake, take some time to think about it, *sí*?'

The light blazed higher in his eyes, his fists lightly bunched at his sides.

Suki nodded because she realised she did need the time. That saying no right then would be diving off a cliff before she'd constructed a safety net.

It was completely selfish, completely delusional, but she wanted to cling to it for just a while longer before it disappeared like mist in the sunlight.

He bent towards her, brushed his lips against her cheek. '*Muy bien.* I'll see you in the living area when you're ready.'

Straightening, he headed for the door, tall, powerful, holding her very life in his hands as he walked out of the room.

Left alone to work through the dizzying highs of imagining his glorious words had been powered by love and the cold lows of knowing the truth, Suki collapsed back against the pillows.

The comforting gesture of sliding her hand over her belly calmed a little of her roiling emotions long enough for the painful but extraneous nuggets to fall away, leaving her with the flags that spelled her reality.

She loved Ramon.

He loved his child.

She would never love anyone else.

Which meant a broken heart was already winging its way to her.

She could run away, wait for the inevitable day to happen and lick her wounds in private. Or she could stay, face it head-on, find a way to move past it while providing her child with the best possible foundation to life?

The thought that she was even considering his proposal sent her back upright, the sheets once again twisting beneath her fingers.

Why not?

She would have to face heartache one day, but was there any reason it had to be right now?

She'd already agreed to co-parent her baby's formative years with Ramon. Just as he'd agreed to restructure his life to suit the baby. And just as they'd gone into conception with their eyes wide open, why couldn't they do the same with marriage?

Because you love him.

Her heart clenched agonisingly. She breathed through it, forcing the pain aside to get to the bare facts. Which were that she would rather spend the next five years with Ramon and their baby than on her own. She would take a single day in his presence rather than do without him.

The inevitable end would hurt like nothing before, but ripping her heart out before she needed to…well, she couldn't…wouldn't do that to herself.

There were no heralding trumpets accompanying her soul-shaking decision, only mild turbulence and the hum of private jet engines.

But she was okay with that.

Rising, she went to the bathroom, splashed water on her face. It took several heartbeats before she could meet her gaze in the mirror. Several more before her conscience stopped berating her for the path she was choosing.

By the time she slipped her dress back on, her head had accepted the decision her aching heart was still struggling with.

Ramon was on his laptop when she entered the main cabin. Seeing her, he rushed to his feet, dark green eyes brimming with purpose and determination snagging hers as he prowled forward.

'I thought you would rest for a while longer,' he said.

There was a definite question in his eyes. A watchfulness that tensed his shoulders and tightened his jaw. 'You asked me to marry you at thirty-seven thousand feet. Rest after that was out of the question,' she half joked.

He didn't laugh. Heightening tension crawled over him as his probing gaze raked her face. 'I suppose you wish me to apologise for ruining your sleep?' he rasped in a low voice throbbing with notes she couldn't define.

Her mouth would've curved in a smile if debilitating emotions weren't see-sawing through her. 'I know how…cumbersome you find those apologies, so—'

'*Lo siento,*' he breathed readily. 'The timing of this could've been better. I realise that now.'

'Oh…okay. What about the timing of my answer? Does now suit or should I—?'

He gripped her arms, which was fortunate because the plane chose that second to dip again. She was thrown against him, her hands coming up to brace against his chest. 'Tell me. Now,' he ordered in a half-growl.

With the moment of truth upon her, the words suddenly dried in her throat.

What in goodness' name was she doing?

But then she looked into his face. His strong, too handsome, enthralling, iron-willed face. Beneath her right hand, his heart beat fast and vigorous. Her own heart tripped over itself. Licking dry lips, she took a deep breath that was nowhere near as steadying as she wished it to be.

'Yes, I'll marry you, Ramon.'

He inhaled, sharp and long, the arms around her tightening for a moment before he nodded. His head lowered.

Suki froze, every cell in her body anticipating his kiss.

But he merely touched his forehead to hers as he said, 'We will succeed in this too. You have my word.'

They wouldn't. Not if he didn't love her. But for the moment, she would fight the demons and bask in that falsehood.

As was its speciality, Acosta Hotel Madrid was also housed in a centuries-old building, this one a towering Renaissance palace taking up a whole block on Plaza de las Cortes.

In honour of its place at the heart of Madrid's cultural heritage, the walls of the vast marble-floored lobby teemed with ancient and modern art. Several of Ramon's own sculptures were displayed in prominent places, with Piedra Galleria Madrid's home situated on the first floor.

As she'd found out when Ramon's assistant contacted her with their itinerary, Ramon chose to stay in private suites at his hotels rather than own homes across the globe.

If she'd thought the Havana version was spectacular, her jaw dropped when she walked into their top floor suite.

Taking up almost a quarter of the whole width of the hotel, the suite was large enough to fit four families with ease. Four adjoining suites and three double bedrooms took up the lower mezzanine floor, with a private pool, extensive living rooms, study and exclusive private spa facilities taking up the floor above it. Signature tones of gold and burgundy themed every elegant room.

As a maid and private butler unpacked their belongings, she stepped out onto the roof terrace, skirting the pool to enjoy the early evening breeze and take in the views and the water display at Fuente de Neptuno.

Ramon found her there ten minutes later, the call he'd needed to make finished. Strong arms planted on either side of her on the terrace wall, bracketing her in. When his mouth brushed the top of her head, her foolish heart soared.

'We have the option of shower and dinner out or swim and dinner in.'

'Hmm, option number two, please. I have the feeling jet lag is just waiting to pounce on me.'

'*Muy bien.* I'll organise it. Before that, you have another decision to make.'

His face remaining cryptic, he caught her hand in his and led her back inside. Two men waited in the living room, one a burly mountain of a man who was clearly a bodyguard. The other was less than half his size, holding a long, thin briefcase connected to his wrist by a chained handcuff.

Ramon exchanged a short conversation in Spanish then indicated the large coffee table in the middle of the room. Still holding her hand, he led her to the sofa and sat her down.

The briefcase was set before her. Opened. It took every ounce of control for her not to gasp.

Some of the biggest diamonds she'd ever seen sparkled from exquisite settings. Rows upon rows of them. Each one bigger than the last.

'You can't stare at them for ever, *guapa*,' Ramon prompted dryly. 'You need to pick one.'

She flashed him a glare. 'Is that *all* I need to do?'

'*Sí*, or you can pick more than one. Make a selection. Decide later which one you prefer.'

'I can't do that!'

He returned her outraged stare with a steady

one of his own. 'You can do whatever you want, Suki,' he stated.

She swallowed hard, the implications of his response settling on her.

She was marrying Ramon Acosta. One of the most eligible men in the world. For whatever time she would enjoy at his side, she would be mixing in the big leagues.

Swallowing jangling nerves, she returned her gaze to the gems on the black velvet tray. Bypassing the more ostentatious stones, she settled on a simple oval four carat surrounded by a smaller ring of diamonds.

When Ramon nodded to the merchant, he stepped forward and made a note of her size. Placing her ring choice in a box, he silently left the room with his bodyguard. The near-silent transaction was surreal.

One she would probably have to get used to, she reminded herself as she slipped off her dress and replaced it with a cream and black striped bikini.

Ramon was already at the pool when she arrived. He watched her approach, gleaming eyes raking over her as she crossed to the lounger next to his. Suddenly self-conscious, she hesitated, then sucked in a breath before she shrugged off her filmy black silk kaftan.

The fevered hiss that left his throat made her breath catch. Jerking upright, he captured her hips, turned her fully to face him before he drew her between his splayed thighs.

'You're showing.' His voice was a little shaken. A little awed. A lot powerful. One hand trailed over her hip to gently trace her belly, eliciting a charged shiver through her.

'Barely,' she whispered.

He shook his head. 'No, I can tell. I can *see*,' he muttered. '*Asombroso.*'

Amazing.

Drawing her slowly, inexorably closer, Ramon placed a soft, gentle kiss on her belly.

The power of it weakened her limbs, stung her eyes with emotions she blinked away hard, even as her heart wept with everything she couldn't have.

Another kiss anointed her. Then another.

When her heart threatened to crack wide open there and then, she stepped back, turned away under the pretext of draping her kaftan on the lounger.

'This baby is going to demand sustenance in T minus half an hour. So I'm hitting the pool now.'

Without waiting for him, she stepped back and headed for the shallow steps, which were, thankfully, on the far side of the terrace, away from his probing eyes. Away from the deceptive bubble that teased her with impossible dreams.

She swam two lengths on her own before he joined her. His powerful strokes easily kept up with her as they lapped the pool, his gaze sliding to her at increasingly frequent intervals.

The moment her arms began to tire, he caught her around the waist and tugged her to the side of the pool. 'You'll not exert yourself,' he murmured into her hair. 'Not even to get away from me.'

Since it was exactly what she'd been doing, Suki thought it wise to remain silent. Or perhaps it was because her vocal cords had stopped working because she was plastered to him from chest to thigh.

Searching for something to take her mind off that thrilling little fact, she asked a question that had been teasing her mind. 'My itinerary shows Dr Domingo and his team are coming in the morning. So they're already here?'

'Yes,' he replied.

'How did you organise that?'

'You didn't want them around, so they'll fly separately.'

Her eyes widened. 'That must be costing you a fortune.'

'A small price to pay for your happiness,' he replied simply, as if they were talking about the price of a latte. But then she realised this was compromise in Ramon's world. She just had to accept it.

Still her breath caught at the ease with which he said that. Then continued catching when his hand slid down her back beneath the water.

'Speaking of which, it's the first ultrasound tomorrow. It's a little early, but I think we both need the peace of mind?'

A different type of zing went through her heart. As if sensing her distress, he tilted her chin with one firm finger. She met piercing green eyes burning with sure fire.

'Everything will be okay.'

'You don't know that.'

'*Sí*, I do,' he said with breathtaking arrogance, as if he had the ultimate power to make it so.

For some reason that worked. Her worry abated and when the butler came out to announce that their dinner had arrived, she let Ramon lead her out of the water. She even let him dry her, let his hand once again linger on the barely there bump.

And when the diamond merchant, who had apparently been quietly working away in one of the suites, appeared halfway through dinner and presented Ramon with a velvet box set on a sterling silver tray, she let the father of her child crouch down next to her at the dining table, slip the stunning diamond engagement ring on her finger and place a firm, lingering kiss on her knuckle.

But, of course, she knew nothing had changed when he escorted her to the guest suite, and walked away in the direction of the master suite.

The following night was the night of the second exhibit. After sleeping in late, she video conferenced with her mother, who was about to start the next barrage of tests, and listened to the expected prognosis with a lighter heart. Carefully avoiding her mother's probing questions about her own situation, Suki finished the call with the promise to visit the next week on their way back to Cuba.

Her own team of doctors arrived just before lunch. Her vitals were taken and her progress pronounced satisfactory before the ultrasound machine was wheeled in.

Ramon, exhibiting not a single ounce of embarrassment, climbed into bed with her and took her hand. The tension in his face echoed hers as Dr Domingo spread warm gel on her belly.

The next five minutes passed excruciatingly slowly, the doctor's perfect poker face giving nothing away. Finally, Ramon snapped, firing bullet-sharp questions in Cuban Spanish at him.

Nods and *sí* were batted back and forth, until Suki too snapped.

'Tell me what's going on!'

Green eyes alight with a fiercely pleased fire locked on hers. 'He says the baby is perfectly healthy and thriving.'

A ferocious shudder trembled through her. 'Oh. *Oh, my God.*'

'I said so, did I not?' he muttered gruffly against her ear.

Her burst of relieved laughter turned into tears. When his strong arms enfolded her she held on tight, the cathartic release of weeks of worry triggering even more sobs.

Their baby was okay.

Maybe they would be okay too.

Several hours later, as she dressed for the event, that hope had taken a firm little root in her heart.

Securing her hair on one side with a discreet silver clip, she arranged the heavy fall over one shoulder. The stylist the concierge had sent up had done amazing things with her eye make-up, the smoky shadow bringing out an extra sparkle that highlighted the joy glowing inside her.

Her baby was safe.

She was still smiling when she answered the knock on her suite door a few minutes later.

Ramon's gaze locked on her face, his body growing stock-still before his gaze trailed a blazing path down her body.

'This dress…*this* one is my favourite,' he muttered.

The red evening gown was a little tighter than when she'd first tried it on weeks ago in Miami, especially around the stomach area where her waist had thickened, but even she had to admit it looked amazing on her.

She smiled. 'I know.'

'But it's lacking something, I think.' He stepped inside, reached into his pocket and brought out a glittering necklace.

More diamonds.

Even more spectacular than her engagement ring. Before she could find the right words to express her shock, he was stepping behind her, securing the priceless jewellery around her neck.

Turning her around, he stared down at her. 'Your pregnancy suits you, *guapa*. You're glowing.'

'With all this bling I'm sporting, how could I not?' she joked.

One corner of his mouth began to lift. The buzzing in his pocket made him draw away from her.

Pulling his phone out of his pocket, he glanced at the screen. And tensed.

'What is it?' she asked.

Tucking the phone against his chest, he traced a finger down her cheek. 'Sorry, *belleza*. I have to attend to some business downstairs. Stay here— I'll be back up in ten minutes to escort you down.'

She started to nod, but he was already walking away. Frowning at his abruptness, she picked up her tiny purse and left her suite.

The butler offered her a drink but she refused, on account of the sudden nerves zinging through her stomach. Unable to settle, she slowly paced the living room. As she passed the open terrace doors a breeze blew in. She shivered, hating the disquieting vibes raising goose bumps on her flesh.

When she heard footsteps behind her, she turned gratefully. Only to be confronted with the last person she expected to see.

Svetlana Roskova was a magnificent vision in white. With her silver-blonde hair perfectly coiled on her crown, her figure-skimming halter-neck dress displaying graceful shoulders and a body that photographers and designers begged for, she was impossible to dismiss.

Bright grey eyes surveyed Suki from head to toe before she glided forward and paused in front of her, her six-foot height on top of her heels making Suki feel like a midget.

'You must be Suzy?' she asked in a smoky voice.

'It's Suki. Can…can I help you?' Suki asked, hating her stumbling voice.

Her smile was shockingly warm. 'Oh, honey, I'm here to help you.'

'I… I didn't realise I needed help.'

'That's okay. I don't mind helping a girl out.' Gliding past Suki, she walked in a small circle, her gaze flitting through the suite. 'I love this hotel. My personal favourite is the Abu Dhabi one, though. Ramon spared absolutely no expense with that one. Which was why it received a seven-star rating, of course. It's also a little less…old-fashioned, shall we say? I don't see the draw in antiques to be honest.' She gave a sultry laugh. 'Which was why I couldn't get the decorators into that mausoleum he calls home in Cienfuegos fast enough.'

Suki gasped, her eyes widening on the supermodel. 'You were the one who changed the rooms?'

For a split second, Svetlana's easy charm dropped. 'He's taken you there, I see.'

'Why are you here?' Suki demanded, the roiling in her stomach predicting unimaginable worst cases.

The Russian beauty moved forward again, her steps faltering when she caught sight of Suki's engagement ring.

'Ah, looks like he's given you one of these.' She held out her right hand, displaying a diamond twice as big as Suki's. 'Did he wine and dine you, then surprise you with a visit from his diamond merchant?'

Suki barely managed to stop herself from gasping again as a hot spike of pain lanced her heart. 'It's none of your business.'

Svetlana shrugged, continuing forward to circle Suki where she stood. From behind her, Suki felt her lean forward. 'He promised me the world too after I got pregnant,' she whispered in Suki's ear.

She felt the blood drain from her head as she spun on her heels to face Svetlana. 'What?'

The icy blonde gave a sad smile. 'Sadly, it wasn't meant to be. And unfortunately, all the silliness started after that.'

'Silliness?'

'Ramon wanted me to quit modelling. Stay at home and try for another baby. I love him but, boy, he's a typical man when it comes to such things. He got his boxers in a twist when I asked for a little more time.'

'Is that why you cheated on him?'

Svetlana's eyes widened ever so slightly, but she recovered quickly. A little too quickly. 'All of that is behind us now. He's forgiven me and now he's got a mini him on the way, there's no reason why we can't be together.'

'Excuse me?'

'Yes, *excuse* you. He's probably spun you a story about how everything will work out with you and him and the baby. But what he hasn't mentioned is that he still loves me. If you think you're going to walk down the aisle with him any time soon, you're delusional. He's keeping you sweet long enough to get his hands on his kid.'

'Why on earth should I believe you?'

'Because *I'm* the one he can't get out of his head. I'm the one he still paints and sculpts when he's in that studio of his. He's as obsessed with me as I am with him. Has been since the first time we met. If you don't believe me, take a peek under all those black cloths in his studio when you go back. *If* you go back.'

'So you came here to what…warn me off?'

'Ramon is waiting for me downstairs so I'll be quick. I came to give you a heads up before you started spinning fairy tales that will never come true. You can either break things off with him or content yourself with being the *other* woman in his life. He'll always belong to me.' She smiled and started heading out of the living room. At the last moment, she executed a perfect pirouette. 'Oh, and don't bother asking him. He'll only deny it. Actually, on second thought, ask him. The quicker we get things out in the open, the quicker we can all settle into our places.'

Suki didn't know where she dredged up the strength to ask one last question, when everything inside her was ripped to shreds. 'Are you seriously saying you don't mind sharing him with another woman?'

She smiled a megawatt smile. 'Woman to woman? I don't because I know he'll always come back to me. When I call he comes running, and vice versa. But I hope for *your* sake you choose the path that causes you least embarrassment and pain.'

With a wriggle of her perfectly manicured fingers, she sailed back out in a cloud of expensive perfume.

Not a care in the world about the life she'd just shattered.

CHAPTER THIRTEEN

SHE WASN'T A CHILD. Or a melodramatic actress in a daytime soap opera, choosing sullen silence or dragging things out for effect.

Even before Svetlana had walked out, Suki knew she would ask Ramon. The need to stop the torture ravaging her insides aside, her assumption that he'd lied to her about his relationship with Svetlana was what had delayed her telling him about her first pregnancy. Condemning him again without concrete evidence would not only demean her, it would erode any possibility of trust between them.

Yes, they had to start from a place of trust so, of course, she would ask him if anything Svetlana had said was true—

'Miss Langston?'

She composed herself and turned to find the butler a few feet away. 'Yes?'

'Señor Acosta called. He's been delayed. He says I'm to escort you down to the gallery and he'll find you there as soon as he's free.'

Trust. Trust.

'I see. Okay.'

The butler smiled.

'Umm, you know what, you don't have to come with me. I know where the gallery is. I'll be fine on my own.'

The older man frowned. 'Are you sure?'

Suki forced a smile. 'Yes.'

Without waiting for an answer, she picked up the clutch, which had somehow dropped to the floor, and walked out of the suite.

Half an hour after she arrived downstairs, Ramon was still nowhere to be seen.

Trust. *Trust.*

But the affirmation was growing weaker because, even though the size of the gallery and the number of guests were almost three times bigger than the Havana exhibition, she refused to believe she and Ramon would've continually missed each other. He wasn't here. Neither was Svetlana. Which meant they were together?

Was it true? Was he so madly in love with Svetlana he would take her back even after she'd cheated on him?

Her soul shredding, Suki continued to look for him. Eventually, she arrived at a set of doors marked *Employees Only.*

Biting her lip, she tried to talk herself out it. Then back into it.

She was the fiancée of the gallery owner. Surely that allowed her inner-sanctum access? The pain ravaged, hysteria-stroking demon inside her gave a mocking cackle.

Hand shaking, she pushed the door open. A wide hallway had two offices on either side, all of which were empty. Suki hated herself for the giddy relief that punched through her as she retraced her steps.

About to walk through the doors, she heard the familiar, sultry laugh. Quieter. More illicit? The sound came from the stairwell she hadn't noticed before. She only took one step before she heard Ramon's deep rumbling voice. Another step onto the landing and she saw them, one floor down. Face to extremely close face.

'I've done what you wanted, Ramon. Now it's your turn,' Svetlana murmured.

'You think it's going to be that easy?' There was a throb of anger in his voice, but also something else. Something spine-chilling.

'She's right upstairs. All you have to do is tell her—'

He caught her by the arms, the move so sudden

it halted her words. The words snarled in thick Spanish were indecipherable to Suki.

'God, I love it when you're so bossy,' Svetlana groaned. She swayed towards him, closing the small gap between them and sliding her arms up his chest. He didn't push her away. Instead he walked her backward until her back touched the wall. Then he braced his hands on either side of her head.

Suki's stomach threatened to flip.

'Svetlana—'

'I've missed the way you say my name, Ramon. So much.'

Suki stumbled back, the black carpeted floor thankfully dampening her footsteps. She had no recollection of returning to the exhibit floor, had no knowledge of how much time had passed. At some point someone must have offered her a glass of champagne because somehow she held one. When she realised it, she quickly set it down.

She couldn't stay here. She needed to leave. Needed to—

'What's wrong, *belleza*? You look pale.'

She whirled around at the urgent demand. Stared at him, unable to believe he was in front of her. Unable to contain the pain ripping her heart apart. Unable to stand that guilty look in his eyes.

Numbly, she shook her head. *Hold it together.*

She turned, spotted Svetlana on the next wall over.

Please. Please. Hold it together. From the dregs of her whittled emotions, she summoned up a smile. 'Nothing's wrong. Absolutely nothing. Did you take care of your *business*?'

He stiffened, his eyes narrowing. 'Yes.'

'Oh. Good.'

Two guests approached. One grabbed his arm. 'Ramon? There you are. We've been searching everywhere for you. Come and meet—'

'Pardon me a moment,' Ramon rasped, ignoring his guests to frown down at her. 'Suki—'

With her last particle of energy, she waved him off. 'It's okay. You're the host. Go and do your thing. I'll find you *if* I need you.'

He didn't fail to catch the stress in her words. His jaw clenched, but, short of being rude to his invited guests, he had no choice but to be cordial.

The hot, ragged breath that poured from the depths of her soul strangled when her gaze locked with Svetlana's.

The Russian didn't need to say one word. Her smug smile said it all.

How she managed to get herself up to the suite and into bed would remain a puzzle to her for ever.

At first she thought she was dreaming when she

heard him call her name. The firm hand on her shoulder woke her into a fresh recollection of her nightmare. Turning over in bed, she stared at the tall form of Ramon cast in half-shadow from the bathroom vanity light. Beneath the drapes, sunlight filtered through.

She sat up, praying there was no trace of the tears she'd shed. 'Yes?' she croaked.

'You left the exhibition without me last night.'

'You were…occupied.'

He took a step closer, reached for her bedside lamp. 'No!'

He froze. 'It's nine in the morning. Any reason why you prefer to converse in the dark?'

Because seeing you will hurt too much.

'I had…have a slight headache.' And a very large heartache. 'What do you want, Ramon?'

'I've been contacted by your mother's doctors. She wishes to speak to you.'

Her heart lurched as she sat up. 'Is she okay?'

'She's having second thoughts about the next course of treatment. They tried to reach you earlier but didn't get through. Nor did I last night.' The question was clear in his tone.

She'd seen his phone calls but hadn't been able to bring herself to answer them. 'I silenced it so I could sleep.'

Reaching for the phone, she flipped the mute button off, still unable to look him in the eye. 'I'd like to call my mother now, please.'

'Suki, we need to talk—'

'I don't want to keep my mother waiting.'

Grim silence met her request. Then he nodded and left the room.

Suki was one hundred per cent sure the sensation zipping through her wasn't relief. For the moment she pushed her turmoil aside and dialled her mother's hospital.

But it wasn't her mother who answered, but the doctor.

'Miss Langston, we think your mother could use some support to see her through this second stage. Are you able to be with her?'

The lifeline wasn't one she wished for but she grasped it all the same. 'Yes. I can be there this afternoon.'

'Excellent. We look forward to seeing you.'

She emerged from her suite after a quick shower and hastily donned jumpsuit and sandals to find Ramon pacing the living room.

As she'd predicted, seeing him in the sunlight, knowing what he'd been doing with Svetlana in the stairwell last night, was almost too much to bear. Every instinct screamed at her to launch into him, but she needed her energy for her mother. 'The doctors think I should be there for my mother. I want to go.'

Brooding eyes watched her for a second before he nodded. 'We'll head to the airport after breakfast—'

'No, I prefer to go alone. I don't want to overwhelm her with company.'

He frowned. 'Suki—'

'The doctors checked me out yesterday. Everything's fine. You're beginning to smother me and frankly I could do with some room to breathe.'

His jaw gritted and his eyes darkened. '*Bueno*. I have a project to finish in Havana for the next few days. You can have that time.'

'Thank you,' she said stiffly.

Breakfast was a silent affair with Ramon eyeing her darkly in between tossing back steaming cups of espresso. The moment she forced down her toast, she stood from the table.

The porter had already headed down with her single suitcase. Behind her, Ramon prowled hard on her fast-clicking heels.

His hand stayed the door before she could open it. When she refused to look at him, he caught her chin in his hand, raised her gaze to his.

Her breath caught at the dark storms swirling

in his eyes. Again she wanted to ask the burning questions that trembled through her. But her mother needed her.

'I'll arrive at the end of the week, Suki. So get as much *breathing* done as possible because come Friday morning, we *will* talk.'

Her hand tightened on her handbag, the alien weight of the ring cutting into her finger. 'I'm sure we will. Goodbye, Ramon.'

He didn't respond, only stared at her for a fistful of seconds before he let her go.

Her body operated on automatic while her mind churned for most of the journey. By the time Ramon's plane landed at London City Airport, she'd worked herself back to her original conclusion. She needed to talk to Ramon, give him a chance to explain. But she was also sure of one thing. Regardless of what he said, there would be no future for them without love.

Svetlana might have thrown a spanner in the works short term but, unless she could find a way to live without Ramon's love, she might be the one to call time on this thing.

The private hospital where her mother was receiving the next phase of treatment in East London was so state-of-the-art, it was almost futuristic.

Her mother was looking much healthier than Suki had seen her in a long time, but minutes after she arrived Moira Langston dissolved into tears.

'Mum, what's wrong?' she asked after handing her mother a box of tissues.

'It's crazy, isn't it? It's only now, when the possibility of getting better and having my life back is in front of me, that I can't help thinking about the past. Don't get me wrong, this infection I've picked up that could derail the treatment is also responsible for my sorry state, but...' Moira shook her head, silent tears filling her eyes.

Suki reached for her hand. 'Everything will be okay, Mum.'

She eyed Suki. 'Will it? Why have you been crying?'

Suki gave a watery laugh. 'Solidarity?' she tried.

'Has it got something to do with that rock you shoved in your bag before you walked in here? Or the pregnancy glow in your cheeks?'

Suki grimaced. 'I wasn't trying to hide anything. I just—'

'Didn't want to worry me. I know.' She paused a beat. 'So what's wrong?'

'I'm in love with him and I'm not sure he feels the same way.'

Her mother's eyes narrowed. 'And?'

The stern voice of the mother who'd taught her self-worth even before she'd learnt to walk straightened Suki's spine. 'And I owe it to myself to make sure I don't settle for less than I'm worth?'

Moira smiled and rested her head on the pillow. 'If nothing else goes right, at least I know I've done all right with you,' she murmured, then closed her eyes.

They had snippets of conversation over the next three days as Moira battled her infection. By Thursday night, Suki was struggling not to show her anxiety.

Ramon had stuck to his guns and given her the breathing room she'd demanded. But it was time to take control of her future once more.

The moment her mother was given the all-clear on Friday morning, Suki kissed her goodbye and summoned a taxi. She toyed with the idea of heading to Ramon's hotel before she discarded it. For one thing, she needed a shower and a few hours' sleep before she could function properly. Turning up at Acosta Hotel London dishevelled and with bags under her eyes would probably get her thrown out before she walked through the revolving doors.

Suki didn't know how sound the decision to go

home was until she stopped at the corner shop to buy a pint of milk.

The sense of déjà vu that engulfed her felt like a tsunami sucking her under as she plucked the newspaper from the stand and stared at the front-page picture.

He was shirtless, the grimy towel he used when he sculpted hanging from the back pocket of his low-riding chinos. She was wearing the kind of long-sleeved *male* dress shirt that strongly hinted at nothing else underneath. Svetlana's miles-long legs were wrapped tight around his waist, her white-blonde hair tumbled in sexy disarray down her back.

And worst of all, they were standing on the terrace of the villa Suki had had the audacity to hope would be her home one day.

The shopkeeper's ever-increasing demand for payment snapped her out of her shock long enough to hand over the appropriate change before she was stumbling down the pavement and into her house.

Lurching into the kitchen, she discarded everything, raced upstairs, flung herself on the bed and pulled the covers over her head.

The thumping came not five minutes later. Or

perhaps it was five hours. She didn't know or care. Nor did she acknowledge it.

Next, her phone began to ring. She ignored that too.

Then the banging started again. 'Open the door, Suki. I know you're in there.'

'Go away,' she screamed.

He went away. Then somehow materialised at the bottom of her bed. 'Get up, Suki. Now,' he growled.

She lurched upright in bed. 'Oh, my God! How did you get in here?'

'I climbed in through the goddamn kitchen window! We're going to have a serious talk about your security when we're done talking about us,' he snapped.

Her world lit on fire and turned to ash again in the blink of an eye. 'There is no us, Ramon. I was delusional in thinking there was a possibility. Trust me, I'm fully awake now to the type of man you are.'

His face paled a little before his mouth thinned into a flat line. 'Because you let that bitch feed you poison or because you've read the tabloids and tried and found me guilty? Yes, I found out she was in the suite. Why didn't you tell me?'

Hot, angry tears prickled her eyes. Snapping

back the duvet, she surged to her feet. 'Because she was there on your behalf. And it wasn't poison if it was true! And don't forget your back-stairwell tryst as well! Did it give you a little thrill to grope her like that while she moaned in your ear? *God, I love it when you're so bossy. I've missed the way you say my name, Ramon. So much.*'

His mouth actually dropped open in shock before he raked his fingers through his hair. '*Santa Cielo*, you heard that?'

She wrapped her hands around her arms. 'I didn't stay for the full performance, if that's what you're asking.'

'Pity. If you'd stayed you would've got the whole picture, instead of the half-baked conclusions you're letting hurt you now. And let's get one thing clear: she wasn't there on my behalf!'

'Don't you dare turn this back on me. You lied to me upstairs when you said you had business to take care of. You lied again when you came back into the gallery, looking *as guilty as hell*.'

'She *was* business, because she turned up uninvited making a nuisance of herself. I didn't want you stressed so I went down there to deal with her. Somehow she slipped past Security and made her way up to the suite. And I felt guilty afterward for neglecting you for so long.'

'Wow, and you rail me about *my* security?' she snapped.

He paced in a tight back and forth at the end of her bed. 'She's…cunning.'

'You mean she's good at getting men to do what she wants, you included?'

'No. I told you, we're over. We've been over for a very long time.'

'There's a newspaper photo and article that says something very different. And don't tell me the picture is false because I recognised the decorator's scaffolding still on the south wall.'

He let out an exasperated breath. 'It wasn't false. She was at the villa two days ago.'

She'd thought the picture that had torn the bottom out of her world had done all the damage she could sustain. She was wrong.

His words sapped the last strength from her legs. Ramon caught her as she swayed. She fought him as he carried her over to the bed.

'*Madre de Dios*, stop this!'

'No. What about you *neglecting* to tell me she was the one who did the appalling redecoration? Or that she was pregnant with your baby, too? You know what? I don't want to do this. Just…just get out of my house!'

'She's lying, Suki. There was never a baby. And I'm not going anywhere. Not until you hear me out.'

Sitting down, he imprisoned her in his lap. Suki sat stiffly, her every cell fighting not to be consumed once again.

'Think about it rationally. You lived in Cienfuegos for almost two months. In that time, did you ever spot a paparazzo there?'

Her mouth tightened but it was clear he wasn't going to carry on until he had an answer. 'No, but—'

'So, why would they suddenly show up, if they hadn't been fed that information?'

'Ramon. It doesn't matter—'

His hand tightened on her hip. 'It matters because she orchestrated it all from start to finish.'

'Because she wants you back that badly?'

He gave a very masculine, very arrogant shrug.

'But that picture. It was...'

'Nothing. Less than nothing,' he insisted.

'Was...was that your shirt she was wearing?'

'I didn't stop to check. It's probably one she took from when we were together. Mario alerted me that there was someone on the premises insisting on seeing me. She launched herself at me out of nowhere.'

Suki shook her head, unable to stop the tears that

brimmed her eyes. With another pithy curse, he took her face in his hands, tilted it up to his.

'Don't do this to yourself, *mi amor.* Can't you see she's not worth it?' he demanded raggedly.

A wet sob bubbled up from her chest. 'I can't get that picture out of my mind.'

'Try. She cheated on me, Suki. But even if she hadn't I doubt that we would've made it to the altar.'

She wasn't going to hope.

She wasn't going to hope.

She...

Oh, hell. Hope bloomed bright and strong. 'You wouldn't?'

He shook his head. 'The initial spark fizzled out very quickly. We both knew it. But she didn't want to admit failure and I initially left it because I felt a little...guilty.'

Her eyes widened. 'Guilty? Why?'

'She overheard me asking Luis about you the day he brought you to the office summer party. Long before we broke up she had a bee in her bonnet about you. She suspected I had a thing for you and she was right. Someone took a picture of us at the Havana event and it made social media. That's what triggered her nonsense.'

Her breath caught. 'You had a *thing* for me?'

'Each time we met I had a harder time getting you out of my head. I think it was partly why—'

'You were so mean to me?'

His low chuckle reverberated through her. 'I couldn't exactly pull your hair.'

'You never know. I might have liked it.'

The humorous moment lingered for a split second before it disappeared under the weight of heavier emotions. 'Ramon—'

His hand tightened in her hair. 'I would *never* cheat on you, Suki. I swear. I love you, only you.'

Her heart stopped, then raced wildly in her chest. Blinking tear-filled eyes, she pulled back, searched his face. 'You love me?'

He squeezed his eyes shut for a second. 'That night after we made love and I left, I couldn't stop thinking about you. I must have picked up the phone at least two dozen times every day to call you. Hell, I may have hated you a little for wrecking my workday for weeks on end. When Luis told me about the pregnancy, my first thought was that I finally had a reason to be in your life. A *permanent* reason.'

'And then it went away?' she whispered.

He leaned his forehead against hers. 'That was one of the worst days of my life,' he whispered back, his gruff voice thick with sorrow.

'I'm so sorry. For both of us.'

'No, I'm sorry. For the way I went about righting what I thought was wrong. You have every right to hate me for the things I said to you. Every right.'

'I tried very hard to save her, Ramon.'

He held her tighter. '*Dios*, I know that now. But losing Luis and my parents on top of losing the baby...it drove me a little insane. I'm not asking you to forgive me now. Just that you'll forgive me some day?' he pleaded hoarsely.

'No, promising to forgive you some day means hanging on to bad feeling now. I won't do that. I forgave you the moment I agreed to have this baby with you.'

Sea-green eyes swimming with heavy, wild, unstoppable emotion met hers. '*Belleza*, I don't deserve you.'

She slid her hands over his five o'clock shadow to cup his face. 'No, you don't, but I'm yours anyway.'

A deep shudder rippled through him. In the next instant, she was on her back, both her hands trapped above her head in one of his as he levered himself carefully over her.

'Tell me again,' he demanded, his mouth hovering a whisper above hers.

'I'm yours,' she whispered fervently.

His free hand trailed down her arm, over her waist to splay possessively over her belly. 'Again,' he growled.

She couldn't stop the tears from filling her eyes again. 'I love you. I'm yours. *We're* yours.'

His own eyes misted as he sucked in a long, unsteady breath. His fingers were equally unsteady as he divested her of her clothes.

He paused when his fingers tangled in her panties. 'The doctors said it was okay, didn't they?'

'They said it was okay *weeks* ago. But you decided to torture us both.'

He grimaced. 'I will make up for that now, *sí*?'

She nodded eagerly. '*Sí, mi amor.* Now and for ever.'

EPILOGUE

Eight Months Later

'*CARIÑO*, WE'RE GOING to be late.'

Ramon thought it wise not to raise his voice above a gentle murmur, seeing as, when it came to this particular subject, his wife was prone to falling apart at the slightest provocation.

That plan backfired spectacularly.

'And whose fault is that?' she snapped. 'Just one picture, you said. No one will notice, you said.'

He winced. 'I'm sorry your pictures turned out to be an international sensation, *guapa*.'

'No, you're not. You crow to everyone who comes within shouting distance that you're my husband. That you're the reason I look the way I look in those pictures.'

'Well…to be fair—'

'Don't you dare. I don't want to hear it. And I didn't want to be the star of your silly gallery exhibit.'

'Okay, then we'll stay home.'

The door to the bathroom flew open. And Ramon was eternally glad he was leaning against the bed frame. Because like always, he struggled to catch his breath whenever he looked at her. The love of his life grew more beautiful each day. She'd become his everything. His wife. His muse. The mother of his child.

His most intense lover.

The sculpture he'd made from the sketches of her on the granite slab had turned out to be too intimate to share with the world, so he'd sculpted another, a mother-son one, which now resided in a special garden at their home in Cienfuegos.

Framed to perfection in the doorway, she flipped golden caramel hair over one shoulder. 'No, you won't cancel. I've already been called a diva for showing up five minutes late to the last exhibit.'

Ramon wisely stopped from pointing out that preventing tardiness was why they needed to leave now. Personally, he wouldn't care if they turned up an hour late, or not at all. But Suki was unused to media scrutiny and still sensitive to being the centre of attention.

Sadly, she'd been thrown in the deep end when the semi-intimate black-and-white photos he'd taken of her with their son had taken the world by storm. Pictures where she'd been breastfeeding, bathing or just taking a nap with Lorenzo. The purity of her beauty had publishing houses clamouring to sign her up to coffee-table portrait book deals.

So far she'd resisted all offers, choosing to only exhibit at Piedra's Havana gallery. Even then, she tore strips off him each time she had to appear in public. But as always, Ramon knew he only needed to get her there. Because the moment she saw the super-sized pictures of their son, her heart melted.

He witnessed that transformation forty-five minutes later as she stood in front of the second to largest picture of all. It was another black-and-white print where she was watching Lorenzo sleep. The awe and love on her face was a shining beacon that was impossible to look away from.

He approached her from behind, admiring her post-pregnancy body draped in a white sleeveless floor-length gown. Sliding his arm around her waist, he breathed in her perfume as she leaned back against him.

'He really is a gorgeous baby, isn't he?' she sighed happily.

'Of course. He's my son.'

She rolled her eyes but turned to bestow a kiss on him. One that lingered and lingered some more until a throat cleared loudly nearby.

Ramon smiled indulgently as his mother-in-law joined them with his nine-week-old son cradled in her arms.

The second star of the show was asleep and gently snoring. But his grandmother couldn't keep her eyes off him. 'He really is a gorgeous baby, isn't he?' she sighed.

They all laughed, Suki's eyes shining extra brightly as they lit on her mother. Moira had come through the cutting-edge treatment with flying colours and been given the all-clear six months ago. With a new lease on life, she'd ditched her job in favour of solo world travel four months ago, only taking a hiatus when her grandson had been born. She was headed to Australia in two weeks and was getting as much time with her grandchild as possible.

Ramon didn't mind. He welcomed the extra time he got with his wife. Moira drifted away to show Lorenzo off to guests, and, almost by telepathy, he and Suki drifted to the largest picture of the exhibit.

Luis was smiling at someone off camera, his young vibrant face turned up to the sun. The teasing twinkle in his eyes was captured for all eternity, something Ramon would be grateful for for ever.

'I miss him,' he admitted gruffly, the pain now dulled with happier memories but never forgotten.

Suki turned from her best friend's image and looked into her husband's eyes. 'Me too,' she murmured. 'I'm so grateful to have known him, albeit too briefly. For the beautiful soul that he was and also because he brought you to me.'

He leaned down, rested his forehead against hers as he was wont to do when emotion got too much for him. When the moment subsided, they walked on, hand in hand, stopping to talk about paintings or conversing with guests.

The sudden clink of glasses stopped her in her tracks. A prominent curator and art columnist whose name she couldn't quite remember was smiling at the gathering guests.

'We've been keeping it under wraps, but, since it'll be in the papers tomorrow, we wanted to formally take the opportunity to announce the formation of the new charity for children's art. It's in honour of Ramon's brother and will be named the Luis Acosta Foundation for Children's Art. Suki Acosta will be its leading patron and has already donated a staggering quarter of a million pounds.'

Rousing applause went through the large crowd. Then she clinked her glass again. 'We also have a special surprise this evening, again, to be announced tomorrow, but I do love letting the cat out of the bag.' She paused for laughter before continuing, 'Anyway, it's my pleasure to announce that the prestigious White Palm Photography Award this year goes to our dear Ramon for the simply named but utterly divine photo known as *Suki & Lorenzo*.'

An image of the very first picture Ramon had taken of her son and her was projected onto the large screen. She'd woken up from a wonderful dream just as Lorenzo too had opened his eyes. They'd been captured staring at each other with eyes full of transcendental wonder and magical hope.

Singularly her most favourite picture in the world; happy tears filled Suki's eyes as she applauded and kissed her husband.

'I'm so proud of you.'

He gave his usual one-sided smile, then caught her hand in his to pull her towards the stage.

'What are you doing? They came here to see you,' she whispered.

'No. You are my true muse because you own my heart. I can't breathe without you, or live without you. I wouldn't want to. So you need to take your bow, *mi amor*, because it's really you they've come to see.'

She stepped up onto the stage beside him, blinking back further tears as more applause broke out. 'Oh, God, you choose the worst moments to say the most wonderful things.'

He gave a very short, very poignant speech, then stepped off the stage and pulled her close. 'I say them because they're true. I say them because I love you. *Dios mio*, I love you so much, Suki.'

'I love you more.'

* * * * *

If you enjoyed
PREGNANT AT ACOSTA'S DEMAND
why not explore these other Maya Blake reads?

SIGNED OVER TO SANTINO
THE DI SIONE SECRET BABY
A DEAL WITH ALEJANDRO
ONE NIGHT WITH GAEL
THE BOSS'S NINE-MONTH NEGOTIATION

Available now!

MILLS & BOON®
Large Print – December 2017

An Heir Made in the Marriage Bed
Anne Mather

The Prince's Stolen Virgin
Maisey Yates

Protecting His Defiant Innocent
Michelle Smart

Pregnant at Acosta's Demand
Maya Blake

The Secret He Must Claim
Chantelle Shaw

Carrying the Spaniard's Child
Jennie Lucas

A Ring for the Greek's Baby
Melanie Milburne

The Runaway Bride and the Billionaire
Kate Hardy

The Boss's Fake Fiancée
Susan Meier

The Millionaire's Redemption
Therese Beharrie

Captivated by the Enigmatic Tycoon
Bella Bucannon

MILLS & BOON®
Large Print – January 2018

The Tycoon's Outrageous Proposal
Miranda Lee

Cipriani's Innocent Captive
Cathy Williams

Claiming His One-Night Baby
Michelle Smart

At the Ruthless Billionaire's Command
Carole Mortimer

Engaged for Her Enemy's Heir
Kate Hewitt

His Drakon Runaway Bride
Tara Pammi

The Throne He Must Take
Chantelle Shaw

A Proposal from the Crown Prince
Jessica Gilmore

Sarah and the Secret Sheikh
Michelle Douglas

Conveniently Engaged to the Boss
Ellie Darkins

Her New York Billionaire
Andrea Bolter